M000076114

THE
SHRIVING
PLACE

A NOVELLA

Brian Patrick Edwards

ROGUS ARDENS

BIRMINGHAM, ALABAMA

Copyright © 2020 by **Brian Patrick Edwards**

All rights reserved. No part of this publication may be reproduced, distributed or transmitted in any form or by any means, without prior written permission.

Rogus Ardens
Birmingham, Alabama
IG: @Cathoholicism

Publisher's Note: This is a work of fiction. Names, characters, places, and incidents are a product of the author's imagination. Locales and public names are sometimes used for atmospheric purposes. Any resemblance to actual people, living or dead, or to businesses, companies, events, institutions, or locales is completely coincidental.

Book Layout © 2017 BookDesignTemplates.com

The Shriving Place/ Brian Patrick Edwards. -- 1st ed.
ISBN 978-0-578-82523-6

Dedicated to the *Good Ones*.

*"As sure as God made black and white, what's
done in the dark will be brought to the light."*
—JOHNNY CASH

CONTENTS

CONCURSUS

Tap—tap-tap

Her fingers tap against my shoulders like a pianist would on keys; I often wonder what sort of masterpieces she's performed on them. Tap—tap-tap-tap they gently patted against my shirt. The little fingers smell of fresh fruit and flowers as the aroma escapes with each additional tap.

She's my Sophia, the youngest of my children, but undoubtedly the most beautiful. Praise be to God she took after her mother. The other two, Eli and Richard, favor me. I shouldn't give the impression that they're hideous; they simply do not have eyes like their mother's. They're prone to stinking and obtaining new stains on their Sunday best. Even as we entered the church, I noticed mud on their knees and broken blades of grass stuck to their shoulders.

Sophia is quite a mess as well, but at least she has a natural perfume about her. The mess she does make is finding what place to put her food in. The little girl hasn't quite figured out the hand to mouth system. She's more hand to nose, hand to cheek, hand to hair and eyes. Mary is good about wiping her clean as she paints her face with food and berry juices.

My wife, Mary, is quite a beauty. The boys would always joke, without lying, that I out-kicked my coverage. I, a neckbearded twenty-something at the time, did just that many years ago. In this very church, perhaps ten, eleven years ago, I first spotted her. I wasn't even Catholic then, but after seeing what such beauty this parish had to offer, you'd think I'd been born with a rosary in hand.

⁎⁎

I felt a calling, you could say, but not in a spiritual sort of way. I had no majestic experience, no angels or trumpets, no Holy Ghost revival, just some kind of realization, I guess. I began to think of my faith in my twenties, why I believed the way I did, why I did the things I did. It was my parents, really, and their parents before them for a hundred years. But what of my ancestors? I'm of broad European ancestry. I found it sorta shameful to not be Catholic, to go my entire life without having been to one of the incredibly decorated churches. That thought was all it took. I made my mind, I would go to my first Mass. I went alone, with not the slightest clue of what to expect. I mean, I did some basic research first, but that's not much, really. I was alien to all the terms, a foreigner to the incense infused rituals and the various marble faces that protruded from every corner of the sanctuary.

Anyway, there she was that very first Sunday, veiled, hidden beneath the delicate white and laced cloth that could only dream of hiding her effectively from me. Her dark curls still managed to find themselves framing her face, a soft, lightly freckled face. Her pale porcelain beauty was clothed in a baby blue dress to match her eyes. I was a savage in this place, gawking at this girl, unaware that I was even in the presence of the Lord. The Bread of Life was broken before me. The people kneeled, yet my eyes were captivated with the dream of her. I followed her every move, did all she did to the best of my abilities. She sat in the pew in front of me, also alone. She held a missal; at the time, I thought it was just a strange little Bible with one too many bookmarks.

I couldn't hear the priest and his incantations. I couldn't hear anything at all. I couldn't hear anything but an extreme silence that I didn't find possible in a room of a hundred people with dozens of babies and elderly. I couldn't hear anything over the soft brush of her dress against the hard-wooden pew and kneelers. Those kneelers were atrocious too, I feel as though they were harsher than the floor itself. These days I kneel on them just for the added penance, but I knew nothing of that then. The praises I would sing if someone had whispered the future with her into my ear that day. It would entail beautiful Sophia, the clones of myself, Richard, Eli, and their dirty pants.

Everyone began lining up. Pew by pew, they emptied out into a line that wrapped itself against

3

the sanctuary's furthest walls. I didn't know what it was; I assumed it might have been Communion. I followed her, ended up right beside her. We kneeled before an altar on the left side of the church. Mother Mary, massive and made of marble, held her ancient arms out to us. She was decorated with a shiny gold heart and a crown of flowers. I always had issues with statues for some reason before, at least when it came to church. I didn't have problems with Mount Rushmore, though, and people travel from all over the world to see those. Mary had no issue kneeling before the statue, so I was fine to follow suit. The priest came to us one by one; I watched him hold out the Bread for my Mary, "Corpus Christi," he said as she opened her mouth and received the Eucharist. I hadn't been hand-fed by anyone since childhood, but I did the same as her and the others. I had no clue that non-Catholics were not allowed to receiver Holy Communion. I had not even researched the Traditional Latin Mass, where I found myself on that Sunday. I had probably only read a little bit about Novus Ordo, the Mass introduced in the sixties. This Mass was the way my ancestors did it, a detail I would be very proud of once I had learned; it seemed proper to me. I followed after her, made the Sign of the Cross as she did. The Mass ended.

She stood from her pew, collecting her things. She had her purse, her missal, or the weird little Bible, I thought. She had car keys with strange medals attached to them, the saints shimmering as light reflected off of them. When she stood, she looked with purpose, direction, as if she intentionally wanted to avoid eye-contact with me. I sprang from my pew, quietly, to follow after her. I didn't want to be a creep, but my attraction to her was far more than magnetic. She stopped abruptly, dipped her fingers into the font of Holy Water, and proceeded to cross herself. I also mimicked this, excitedly drowning my fingers in the font, soaking them, soaking my forehead and shirt with the Holy Water as I crossed myself backward. Backward as the Eastern Catholics do, but I wouldn't know that for a long time. I wanted after her. I wanted to possibly talk. Perhaps God would work a miracle for me, but she was gone. She vanished within the blinding sunlight that flooded the usher-held doors.

I would have another chance, I thought. Good women like her always returned to church, like gulls to the shore.

As I hold Sophia in the cry-room, I find myself in those times, dragged into the depths of my mind by the untouched surroundings of the church. The ceiling seems to almost stretch as far into Heaven itself, opening unto us all the beauty that must be hidden behind this thin veil of life. There are angels and saints up there, painted upon the blue and maroon tiles. The saints pierced and cut, with daggers and spears perpetually fixed into their skin. Towards the front of the sanctuary is an enormous mural of Christ with vines leading to Him. He holds before Him the Eucharist. Underneath him stands a massive high altar, which there aren't very many of these days.

After Vatican Two, the Church in Rome developed a taste for iconoclasm; Some say to appeal to the Protestants, or because the Church became infested with Marxists, Freemasons, or Jews. Who knows? Pick your poison and hate it. That's a reason I like this particular church so much. It's untouched. The building was built a hundred years ago. It was built the right way; they don't make them like they used to. Nowadays, you'd be subjected to blank walls. Nowadays, you'd find yourself in a parish seemingly no different from a southern Baptist church, maybe with two or three statues hiding somewhere. It's interesting that this church would be found in the heart of Protestant Mecca; that's my name for the Bible Belt.

Oh, Birmingham, you lovingly bloody city; your history is wet with the blood of many, and you smoke from bombings and burned crosses. There's a Cathedral downtown; a priest was shot on the front porch there in the Twenties. He had done a secret marriage for a Puerto Rican and some white girl; the dad wasn't pleased about that. That cathedral was absolutely gutted after the Second Vatican Council. You'd think they'd leave a martyr's church untouched. Father Coyle was his name, he's not canonized as a Saint, but you'd think the local Church would treat the belongings of the Cathedral as if he was. I don't think they even kept the porch he was shot on the same. Sad. If he woke from the grave today, he'd probably have to ask for directions to his very own cathedral's bathroom. He was one of the Good Ones too. I noticed that pattern of recent history; the Good Ones die, the Perverts seem to escape all confinement of reality. A priest married your daughter off to some slightly brown man? It's okay. He's on the porch, go shoot him. A priest molested your daughter? Oh well, he's gone. He's been relocated far away.

I shouldn't speak of such things, but these are my thoughts. My thoughts as they are in the holiest of times at Mass, Christ have mercy on me. I notice I'm holding Sophia too tightly. I get caught up sometimes.

Don't think it was Sophia, by the way. Our priest here is a Good One; he speaks Latin. It wasn't my daughter that was abused. No, the little girl who was abused didn't have a father around. She was an angelic thing too. I used to wonder why such horrible things happened to the gentler things, but then I remembered Christ; I look around and see martyrs all over the ceiling. People often ask, "if God is real, why do bad things happen?" If evil isn't real, then why do such horrid things happen to the purest? If there is such evil, such dark, abysmal evil engrossed by the brightest objects, then that says something, doesn't it? There's something out there that hates goodness, and God is the source of all good things.

Anyway, it's my personal mission to remove evil from this world. I'm a sort of traveling salesman. I sell biomedical devices to different hospitals in many cities. I meet a lot of people, sometimes I'm the last person they meet.

BRIAN PATRICK EDWARDS

EGRESSUS

Today is Monday. It's another time I must leave, and I'm flying to New York City. There's a hospital in Long Beach interested in a deal for three-hundred and fifty machines that watch people die more accurately. I stand in my open closet, looking for my shoes. I packed them away last night, yet they've made themselves scarce and missing from my luggage.

"Have you called Tommy back?" My wife asks, turning over in bed. It's early; the children haven't begun yet. Sophia is the family's alarm clock; when she cries, it's time for everyone else's day to start. She's typically more like a rooster, shrieking as early as five, but we really wore her out last night while playing.

"No, not yet."

"When are you? I don't know how long you exp--"

"Please, Mary, I just haven't yet." I interrupt what I already know she's after. I calm my tone, "I know."

"The kids really miss you. I miss you."

I respond with the same sentiment. I kneel down and look under the pile of high heels and sandals to search for my shoes with no luck. I stand again and sit on the bed next to my wife. I begin to pet her frizzy bed-made hair. She's clearly upset, wanting to continue her plot for me to change jobs. She's tired of me being gone so often; the business has taken me further away for more extended amounts of time. I've secretly loved those particular details, but I do miss my children. I really do. I miss them and our far too few family nights, but the *jobs* are crucial.

"I think the boys took your shoes last night. Have you checked their room?"

"I'll check."

"They don't want their daddy leaving."

"I know."

The boys are sneaky. They're nothing but noise in the day but apparently get by silently when I'm sleeping—what a horrifying thought. I walk to their room that's down the hall and on the other end of the house. Their soft breaths draw in the cool air in unison. I don't see my shoes on their floor or in the dressers. I look over their dimly lit beds. Richard has his back to me, and Eli seems to be holding something. I look closer in the dark lighting, and I see a slight reflection from the shiny brown shoe. I gently tug it from his tired fingers. He doesn't move. I assume that each boy has their own shoe. Richard will be more difficult, his back is turned, and he's probably cradling the filthy thing. He is. I was hoping not to wake them. I said goodbye last night, but I've got a flight to catch. My plane leaves in a little over an hour. The shoe's shape is apparent through the sheets. Richard was clever. He made every attempt to ensure I would wake him.

"No! Daddy, please stay."

"Shhh-shh-shh." I snag the shoe from his grip and pet him with my other hand. "I have to go."

Eli lifts his head and looks around for *his* shoe, which I've already taken.

"Why? Why can't you work from home? Get a job like mommy?"

"Your mother's job is to be a mother. Someone has to make money for us, for y'all's food, for this house you live in." I bend down between them both, "It's a man's job to hunt and provide. A long time ago, men would be gone far away, looking for food. They'd travel to cities and sell just like I do. If there was war, they'd often go away for years even." Their eyes begin to open wider; history is exciting to them. "Odysseus went to war for ten, and it took him just as long to return home. Daddy will only be gone for four days. We've got planes now. I won't be gone long at all." They like to think daddy is off hunting or at war with Trojans. It's all romance and adventure to them.

"I love you, dad." Richard says, reaching forward to hug me.

"Please," Eli begged, "don't take as long as *odisus*."

I hug them both, and we laugh. "Now, go back to sleep boys, it's still very early. Wait for mom to wake y'all up."

I leave them and silently pass by Sophia's closed door, careful not to make any noise. Sometimes, if the house remains quiet enough, she'll sleep until eight. It would be nice if Mary got the break. I do feel guilty leaving the kids entirely to her for such long periods of time. It's difficult, but she could always call in some grandparents. She doesn't like having them over to a dirty house, and by dirty, I mean the ceiling fans haven't been dusted this week, and there's three dirty glasses in the sink. She's very particular about cleanliness; some may call her obsessive. I stop by our bedroom once more on my way out. She's on her phone, likely reading through a blog of her's.

"The boys had your shoes, didn't they?"

"Yes."

"I heard them rummaging around after you went to sleep. I thought their effort deserved the payoff. Sorry."

"I told them to go back to sleep. You should sleep longer."

"No, I think I'll get up for some coffee and laundry. I'm not sure I can fall back asleep in this empty bed anyway."

"Four days. I'll be back in four days."

"Call Tommy."

I lean forward across the bed to give her a smooch. Her lips are warm, as she is still warm in the bed. The air is cold, and I think of how wonderful it would be to climb into the sheets again and nap for a while. I withdraw instead and pack my shoes along with my other things.

"Get my mother a coffee mug. Buy the kids something as well."

"Of course. I love you, Mary."

"I love you." I leave her to her morning of cleaning.

*
**

My plane boards in thirty-five minutes, but really that's plenty of time. The Birmingham airport is dead, always. It was supposed to have been the HUB that Atlanta is, but the leadership here preferred quietness, I guess. I used to hate that about them when I was young. I wanted the thrill of liveliness in the city, but those things are overrated. Short security lines are much better. Driving fifteen minutes across town at ninety miles per hour with zero traffic at five in the morning is so much better. I was always impatient and had a lead foot, even in a place that requires very little waiting for anything. It doesn't take long for me to find myself sitting at the desolate terminal. For the next few hours, my mind is free to wander.

Tommy is a cousin of mine. He's recently started selling insurance and talks a lot about how easy it is and how awesome he thinks I'd be. He says they're frequently hiring too, but there are no benefits. I'm an incredible salesman, so sufficient that my friends call me The Jew. There's not an ounce of Ashkenazi in me. I even had the DNA done for a bet they had. They still don't accept the results. They think I'm full of "Jewish Magic," as they call it. They say I use Talmud wizardry. I don't know anything about that. I'm just good at selling, but I don't want to change jobs. The insurance job does not have the same perks as mine does.

It's a sort of Catch-22, really; I hate leaving my family, but I love the opportunities it gives me. I get to visit so many different churches. I get to shake hands with all the LGBT-promoting priests and all the other strange species of Jesuit, from the in-hiding to female-priests advocates. They're treacherous, but they're the only ones that I ever confess to.

My time to board has come. I have a carry-on. It's just a bag with my laptop in it, some leather journal I never actually write in, and Holy Water. Everything else got checked in.

I take my place at a window seat on the plane out of habit. The aircraft is mostly empty. I don't even look out of the window hardly anymore. I used to love that as a kid; it's nice if I know to be looking for something. I've spotted Half Dome from the air once; I was proud of that one. The grand canyon was easy to see. Just look for Mars where Earth should be. Mary and the kids traveled with me on that trip. I didn't *stretch my legs* then like I do now. It was their first visit to the west coast. It was pleasant, other than explaining every error of the people that live there.

That actually pisses me off quite a lot; why do all the paradises in this life become infested with the most degenerate people? Everywhere that's pretty and happens to have conservative inhabitants is a miserable sweat factory. Someone once joked that God gives the tolerable climates and paradises to the wicked because they won't have that once they're done here. Maybe that's just true in America, I don't know.

"Good-morning."

I look up from my blank-paged journal. A tall man is packing his carry-ons into the overhead compartment. He's covered in dark black hair and has salt and peppered stubble over most of his red-brown face. Something is a bit distinct about him. I fly a lot. I'm unsure if he's someone that knows me or if he's an actual *stranger*. Perhaps we've shared a flight before.

"Good-morning," I say.

He sits down in the aisle across from mine. I don't know why, with the plane being so empty. He could sit literally anywhere else. It sort of frustrates me.

"You headed to the Big Apple today?" He asks.

We are to change planes in Milwaukee. It's strange he'd assume that immediately. He puts me on edge. What if he's an agent of some sort? FBI? Something else, maybe? Should I know him from somewhere? I hope I'm not forgetting someone.

"Yes, actually. I have some work there in a hospital. Yourself?" I relax a bit. There is no reason I *should* be anxious. I'm your typical salesman—a boring traveling salesman with a wife and three kids.

"Ah, I see." He fools with a bag of chips, looks at the ingredients, squinting his eyes in confusion. "I'm headed there for some consulting. A friend of mine has been making a mess in his affairs. I'm gonna talk some sense into him."

"Ah, well, hope it works out."

"Probably won't. He's a bonehead." The large man puts the unopened bag of chips away and brings out an eye mask. He puts it on his shaggy head and over his eyes, "Be a pal and wake me up if I don't."

I return to the empty journal pages before me. The pen hovers over the spotless lines. I'm not afraid of him reading what I have to say. After all, he does have his eyes covered, but I'm also one of those freaks that made a secret alphabet when I was a kid and happened to stick with it all these years. I guess someone could decipher it if they really tried, but they'd probably have to work at it for a while. Words like *the, and, I,* are all attributed to a unique character. Those sorts of words make it easy to crack simple codes. When I was a kid, I spent so much time developing this little language that it made more sense to keep it. I had no intention of harboring any secrets, but I'm glad because I have nothing but secrets, it seems.

I begin to write. There's no turning back now. The untouched journal has been dirtied with hints of my sins and my reasoning for them. I don't blame anyone; it's not anyone's fault. I guess you could blame me entirely, but I only exist to extinguish what should have already been snuffed out. In a just society, I wouldn't be in this position. The matters I deal with should be no business of my own, yet the world makes them so because the world isn't just.

In the journal, I started back years ago. It all begins in that same church that I found Jesus, that I found Mary. "To Jesus through Mary" is what a lot of Catholics say. I believe the same, do not mistake my humor for disrespect. I just had two Marys in my case.

I went back the following week to that church with the beautiful veiled girl. I sat in the same place as I did before, and so did she. We didn't speak. I went back the next week for a third visit, and the results were the same. I had the Body of Christ many times when I shouldn't have had Him. The fourth time, I beat her to Mass, and I sat in her spot instead. She still sat a row ahead of me. I worked up more courage that fourth time. I nudged her shoulder while the Rosary was being prayed before Mass.

"Excuse me."

She turned and looked at me, her face partially out of sight from beneath the lace veil. Her eyes peered through to my very heart. She seemed almost frightened, or maybe startled.

"Do you mind if I follow along with you?" I smile, "I'm sorta new, and after several weeks I still don't know what's going on."

"I guess that's alright." That was the first time I heard her voice. Previously, I had only heard it in unison with others during the prayers. It had been like tasting the icing on a cinnamon roll. You know it's sweet, but the flavor is lost with the rest of the pastry. Before, her voice was drowned out in all the others', but now I could hear it for what it was, like dipping your finger in the icing and tasting it directly. Her voice was delightful, with a warmth to it that melted into every word.

"Don't feel like you have to, I-"

"No more talking, come sit with me."

I sat with her and watched her pale fingers with baby-blue painted nails. They led my eyes across the Latin. Then I watched when she revealed the English translation on the other side. It came time for Communion.

"Are you Catholic?" She asked quickly. I was already standing behind her, waiting for her to lead to the Eucharist.

"I don't know, I guess?" I said. I didn't want to turn her off. I didn't want to be a heretic, heathen, or whatever name they had for me. I liked Catholicism. I had really enjoyed some of the Saints over those weeks between Masses. The question seemed so definite as if I had skipped over some things that no one had informed me of.

"Stay here. Don't receive." She demanded as she turned to leave. I was disappointed. I felt like a dog, thrown out of the warmth of a bed. Did I have flees? Was it my odor? She looked back to make sure I stayed. I didn't know to kneel either without her. I looked around for the guidance of others now that she had left me. I kneeled, seeing a man across from me doing so—the same dreadful kneelers.

I waited for the communion to be over, kneeling for what seemed an eternity. Good grief, my knees were uncomfortable on those hard kneelers. They clearly had a cushion to them, at least by the sight of them, but it felt similar to pressing your knees into the corner edge of a two-by-four. I looked around, hoping to find someone in discomfort but saw no one. Children were kneeling, old men, and morbidly obese women that seemed to have absolutely no problem with the horrible little kneelers. I felt humiliated. Was I soft? I was.

She returned to our pew, kneeling, and began praying silently. What marbled face was she praying to? Which tortured Saint was it that had their ears held out for her? Was it the Mother of God? How does one get the audience of her's, would she not be busy? Curiosity was my prescription for whatever pain those damn kneelers caused. I hadn't known then, but the Eastern Catholics stood during their Liturgy; I would have much-preferred standing for two hours than this discomfort.

The Mass ended shortly afterward. I was in luck that Sunday. Apparently, there was a lunch-time feast waiting to be served in the basement. I didn't know beforehand, the priest had mentioned it, but I wasn't paying attention to him.

"Are you hungry?" She asked.

"Yes." I lied. I was hoping it was an invitation for more time with her. Maybe I would learn a name. I would acquire the name to beg God for.

"I'm Simon."

"My name is Mary." She smiled.

Ding-ding-ding, the comms alert, I stop writing in the journal. I had covered several pages in the silly scribbles of mine.

"Please remain seated and check that your belts are fastened. We are preparing to land, do not remove seatbelts until the indicator that's lit above you turns off."

We circle Milwaukee for fifteen minutes. The bearded *pal* beside me seems to drool. It's easy to wake someone. It's difficult to wake someone that's drooling.

Ding-ding-ding, the seatbelt indicator turns off.

"Welcome to Milwaukee. Thanks for flying."

ORA ET LABORA

Tap-tap-tap

I poke harder, he's not responding to my tapping finger. Sophia wouldn't have a chance waking this guy up, maybe not even with her 5 AM screeching. The grungy man turns his head away from me.

"Hey pal, we've landed. Wake up." I push much harder. I want to slap him across the back of his head. That would wake him.

"I'm awake."

"Good. We have another flight to catch. Get up."

"I'm up, I'm up." He lifts his golden sleep mask, rises, and removes his things from the overhead compartment. He starts to walk off ahead of me.

I don't like this grungy man. I'd like not to have met him. I could walk much faster than him, but it's too awkward leaving him behind, considering we're going to the same place. With my luck, he'd sit directly across from me to scold and mock the fact that I have no patience.

The airport is filled with different people. Airports are always filled with unfamiliar people. In Birmingham, perhaps because I know I'm home or anyone who gets on there is a native, but elsewhere is always filled with strange-looking groups. The gene pools are unusual, I guess. I've never quite put my finger on it. There are different noses, different jawlines, the cheeks sit higher or wider, the cheekbones that is. The people are shaped distinctively. I'm not speaking about the foreigners; of course, Asians and Arabs look different. No, I'm speaking of the white people. I assume it's because other groups immigrated here initially. I don't know. Maybe they're more German?

We walk silently near each other to our terminal. This airport is much busier, or as busy as an airport should be. The world has woken up by now. The sunlight blazes through each window, illuminating all the dust and debris, everyone's shared dandruff, and fuzz floats in the air above. We really do return to dust. We're not much more than that.

This flight is packed out, yet the sleepy man is sitting nearby. I can see his gigantic fuzzy head bobbing a few rows ahead. He's an invasion of everyone's personal space. Luckily, none of my new neighbors have acknowledged my existence. I'm invisible, and so are they. They stare boringly into the air with their fat faces and decades of wrinkles.

It's a long time before we were in the air. I liked things much better during the Coronavirus, with everything empty. Places were easy to navigate. People weren't around to get confused about their seats and to pack their carry-ons correctly.

I bring out my laptop and skim through the news. I feel like journaling more, but writing in a code is pretty embarrassing, if I'm honest, and I don't want my neighbors gawking at it.

There's been some fascinating headlines this year. Priests are being murdered, but some are looking more like suicides. The investigators aren't talking much about it. Some say it might be depression and violence caused by social distancing. A priest in San Francisco is found in an alley. A few months later, one from Miami, and so on. I'm sick of them being treated like martyrs by their cult-followings. None of them were martyrs. They weren't Good Ones.

What's funny are all the theories behind it. The average person may think they must be hate crimes or attacks on Catholics in general, probably performed by some Muslims. Others believe it's some New World Order plans afoot.

Still, what a joy it is to see less of their opinions too. The radio silence that has been building is such a great relief from the constant revisionism plaguing this era. It's not silent enough. There are still new ideas. There are new rising stars to fill the void of missing heresy. I don't think I'll ever be done. I don't know. I didn't really plan on ever being done, but I often miss the simplicity.

I take this time to research the next priest that may end up like the others. He's a Bad One too. He's an apologist for gay marriage and allows the perspective that such marriages will be done within the Church, by the Church, eventually. He never quite says anything to discourage that idea; he never corrects it. I know he has demons. He must, especially considering he's helped exonerate perverts. People that are on that front are always looking forward. It's not a question of gay marriage, which shouldn't be a question whatsoever, but it's a question of what's next?

How far is culture from pedophilia? How long before people aren't even apologized to? It's a natural sexual preference, they will say. It's beyond our realm of understanding. They're not evil; they're humans too. They make TV shows sexualizing children, and the devils come out to defend them. The Blue Checkmarks aren't hiding their opinions, but broadcasting them for all to read, for all to agree, eventually. The hivemind is at work, and the general population is receiving their updates. They will comply with every disgusting thing they put out. The Bad Ones will be there to guide religious down such a dismal road as well.

I think maybe one day, I will be done. At the rate the world is going, we are due for a collapse. Morals always go first. It's like an air balloon; you can only cut away so much weight.

Father Davis McKinney, a Jesuit; He's a sort of big fish in the world of homoheresy. He has everyone convinced that God makes people gay. People then assume that if God makes you a certain way, then God wants you to behave that particular way, that it's God's blessing to pursue happiness. I want to be clear, God does not make you a sinner. God does not make you gay any more than He makes you a pedophile. The world does that. Abuse does that. You do that.

The guy beside me has begun to snooze. I can get to journaling once again.

*
**

She felt spiritually responsible for me ever since I asked for directions to Heaven. I didn't understand the Mass and had committed some abuses here and there to the Body of Christ that I wasn't even aware of. I was a barbarian crashing the Heavenly Feast. We would sit together every Sunday, and it was delightful, but she had her guard up. She wouldn't budge, but she was gorgeous and yet smart on all things. Mary was and is still an outstanding Catholic; she has all the practice down and the reasons why.

It was after Mass one of those Sundays that we sat together. We would watch the Priest clean and put out envelopes for offerings in the pews. We would help him as often as we could as well. Mary got the broom, and I steadied the dustpan, collecting all the dirt that people carried into that Holy Place. So much dirt, we're not much more than that.

"So, what do you do?" I asked as I watched the fine line of dirt that formed against the brim of the pan. Some of it simply wouldn't pass into the pan. It would collect and resist each passing sweep.

"What do you mean? Like for work?"

"Yes, for work." I still had a vague clue who or what Mary even was. She had been only Catholic, but I knew there was a Mary beyond the parish walls.

"I work at a daycare."

"Oh, you like kids?"

"Of course."

"Does that not wear you out?"

"Depends on how good the help is. The daycare is pretty large, and we have loads of workers, but sometimes I get paired with some that are pretty useless."

"Am I a good help?" I asked, waving the dustpan in the air; she laughed.

"Yes, you're much better help than some of those women."

"And what do you do when you're not working or praying?"

She had a blank look on her face.

"I guess I do a whole lot of nothing. I work nine hours, go home, read maybe, watch TV, talk to my friends online. I don't know."

"Girl, we need to get you out of the house."

"Why?"

"Life is more than working and praying." I dumbly said, utterly unaware of ora et labora.

"Is it?" She laughed.

"Yes, I think so. We make money to live. We should live, sometimes at least."

"Living is too expensive."

"Going to the park is free."

"Ora et labora."

"Carpe diem!" I said.

"Saint Benedict said ora et labora."

"I don't know who said carpe diem."

"Well, working and praying is the easiest way to live a saintly life. It cuts out all the sin. You can't sin or offend God if all you do is work and pray."

"You'd have to really work to be an offense to God, Mary. You're a pretty spotless person. I don't think it's possible."

"I'm not perfect."

"Pretty darn close." Came an Irish voice. It was the priest, laughing as he jabbed at me. He only jokingly made the voice. He had Irish roots but was no more Irish than the pubs downtown.

"Oh, Father, you should know I'm a sinner."

"It's all nothing. I hear all sorts of things. I hear horrible, horrible things every week, from dozens of mouths. Mary, almost full of grace." He laughed.

"Father," I began, "how does one convert?"

"By mopping." He laughed again while he opened the janitor's closet. He rolled out the empty yellow bucket with a filthy mop that sat in it.

"You really want to convert?" Mary asked excitedly.

"Yes."

"Why?" The priest asked, winking at me. He knew Mary probably had a large part in it.

"Seems like a nice alternative to Hell."

"Worked for me." The priest laughed. He was always laughing. I don't understand how someone could face the madness of unmasked humanity every day and still find hope and joy.

"So?"

"Do you have proof of a Christian baptism?"

"Proof?"

"Have you been baptized?"

"Yes. Probably about three times." The priest rolled his eyes.

"Well, surely you managed to get a certificate at one of them, at least?"

"I don't remember."

"Do you know what church it was?" I nodded, "Well, if you give them a call, I'm sure they'll have a record of one of them. Bring me a copy of one, and I'll work with you."

He ran off to some other work and left us with the mop and bucket. The church wasn't gigantic, but the floor space seemed so. It was so much floor. The ancient tiles didn't look any cleaner as the mop passed over them. The age only shimmered beneath the murky mop water.

I liked the age of the church, don't think I'm not a fan of it. Newly built churches are too clean; the walls are blank and cheap, like set-pieces. The old church was made by a hard-working class of Americans and immigrants who have long been put to rest. Even during its building, amid the Great Depression, work did not stop. People still cared about God when their wallets and stomachs were empty. They slaved away to build something that allows the mind to travel to Heaven Itself. The age didn't bother me; there was and still is something magical about it all. I thought of all the souls that left their dust and sins behind on the path to Heaven. It seemed almost sinful to clean too hard. Mary didn't seem to understand this when I'd talk about it later on; she wanted the church to be spotless as Heaven. I'd tell her that we'd never be able to afford golden floors and pearled doors.

"I've got to get going." She said. We had only finished mopping the major traffic areas; I guessed that's all we really needed to do that night, but I wasn't ready to say good-bye for the week.

"Where has the time gone?" I flipped out my phone. It was dark outside; the time was close to seven.

"That's how it goes. Thanks for helping today. We don't always need to clean so much, just once a month."

"Well, would you like to get dinner? My stomach's been growling for the past hour."

"I know, I've heard." She laughed, "But I can't. I've got some things to get to back home." It just sounded like an excuse to me; it most certainly was. I didn't mind if she didn't want to eat that night, but I really desired the extra time with her.

"I'll walk you out."

"Don't be silly."

"How's that silly? We're in the hood." I hadn't thought of that until then. We were on the westside of Birmingham after sundown. It seemed almost irresponsible that the priest would even allow her to clean this late. "Does the priest not realize this?"

"We usually clean on Saturdays in the morning or at noon. The other women are on a retreat, so it was just last minute today, I guess, and I didn't keep track of the time."

"I see. Well, let me walk you out to your car then."

She seemed a bit uncomfortable. I didn't know what it was. Maybe she was worried about going out there. I assumed she wasn't aware of the danger until I had mentioned walking her out. It wasn't simple chivalry on my part; Birmingham has always been one of the top cities for violent crimes per capita. Though, I'd even walk her out had we been in the suburbs. She was too beautiful, too pure, she was a light for all the wicked to attract to, like the insects they were.

"Okay."

I led her out the doors and into the dimly lit darkness with sparsely placed halogen lights. The orange glow resembled Hell after we exited the church filled with saints and the incense-stained air. I walked with her as she quickened for her car. Sirens in the distance howled, and I had my head on a swivel; every shadow seemed intent on violence. She unlocked her car, and I reached to open it for her.

"I've got it." She snapped as she cut past me. She was suddenly angry.

"I'm sorry. Would you like me to drive behind you?" I asked as she sat down in her car. I thought of all the hijackings and kidnappings. What if she needed to stop for gas? What if she became lost? I worried.

"No."

"Please?"

"No!" She slammed her door after cranking the car.

I was dumbfounded. I didn't know what had happened. The entire day had seemed to go nicely, but I was abandoned in that parking lot. I wouldn't chase after her. I didn't want to seem like a creep. Maybe I had freaked her out, I thought. I wanted to talk to the priest. I needed to give him a piece of my mind.

ADVENTUS

The *cesspool* is hard to paint in words, although it's covered in so many advertisements and brands. I've been here before, and every time it's the same feeling I had on my first visit. The buildings scrape along the sky and are so tall that they almost seem to stand directly over you, tilting to cover all sight of blue. It's concrete claustrophobia made with packed people, smoke, cars, and the proud faces of shiny blue glass. Somehow, there's a presence to it as well, a sort of dark feeling I have. It's something cold and wicked in the air, a sound that never leaves the ears.

The older buildings are adorned with gods of the ancient world. They're the pagans' patrons of wheat and harvest, forever standing over a city void of farms. They're gods of plenty in a realm of hunger, unable to bend their concrete arms to the beggars that chant just below them for money.

Ideas are being shouted from every corner, none of them agreeable to me. Black Hebrew

Israelites condemn my race to Hell, even the two percent of my sub-Saharan DNA. The liberal white Christians ramble mindlessly about God as if they're experts after never attending church. I never understood why they insist on making themselves authorities on morality. They don't think of decency, not really. Their brains are sponges for celebrity opinions and television programming. They eat out of a pig's trough of partial philosophies. It's just a place packed with everything, yet empty. I'm happy to be getting out of the city. I prefer Long Beach much more. It's a weird sort of place.

The flight was gentle. At some point, after we landed, the annoying grungy man had vanished. I was almost afraid he'd want to make plans since we were from the same place. After we all left the plane, we found ourselves in a bustling airport. There were so many people. So much noise. I still feel as though I'll bump into him, or perhaps he's following me in some way. What if he was investigating me? Maybe I'm only being paranoid.

My grandmother was paranoid. She had schizophrenia. That's always eaten at me in the back of my mind. There's a bit of that somewhere in me, waiting to be broken like an egg. The right amount of a bad thing and the schizophrenia would surely crack my mind open and spill out my inherited insanity. I'm more afraid of it now, considering my *job*. It's probably not a good job for me, but someone has to do it. Someone has to help hold the dustpan and collect all the dirt that's in the world.

It's such a shame. It infuriates me that *he* has already been collected. *The Bad One*, the reason why I do what I do. Time drew his number, and he answered as all old disgusting, perverted men do. I wasn't there to call his number, but I will for many more.

The priest in Long Beach, *Father* Davis McKinney, is making posts on his social media. His number will be called soon. The thrill of the hunt is setting in. He's tagging his locations in a Church not far from where I am now. How wonderful the world would be if I could simply walk into that church now and end him. Life's more about games, though. It's more about rules. You can't just walk up to a rectory these days and blow him away. No, people don't like games with so few restrictions. They make laws. You have to hunt him down in the cover of night. Follow him. Call his number quietly, so no others hear it called.

*
**

Ring-ring—ring

I look over the cracked surface of my ringing phone. That crack was done on the last hunt. A little bit of a reminder, it taught me to make a checklist of things not to leave on a worksite. Had it slipped from my pocket and onto the floor of the dead priest? That would not work out well.

The face on the screen is of my wife. I texted her earlier and told her I had made it to New York. She's wanting to do a video-chat. I answer.

"Hello, lovely." She's in our kitchen, holding Sophia, who greets my face on the screen with uncontained excitement.

"Look who it is, Sophia! Da-da!"

"Da-da-da-da-da!" Sophia's mouth repeats with a line of drool hanging, dripping onto her lunch-time bib.

"Hey girl," I smile, "What are y'all up to?"

"Just got done eating," it's hard to hear her over Sophia's screeching, but I can overhear the boys shouting from a nearby room in the background.

"I'm just about to eat as well. Getting a slice of pizza."

"That sounds so good."

"Too bad Sophia isn't here to demand tithes from my plate." I joke, whenever we have pizza at home, the little girl always begs for small pickings from our plates by slamming her hand on the table. Mary typically ends up feeding her all the best parts of her own slices.

"Lucky you."

"Where are the boys?"

"They're chasing after each other. They've been at it all day."

"I wanna see them too."

"Boys, your father's on the phone. Come say hi."

It only takes a moment before they run up beside her at the table. They're panting and red in the cheeks. Richard's hair is wet with sweat, sticking to his forehead.

"Hey, dad!" They grin.

"Y'all behaving for mom?"

"Yes." They lie. Mary rolls her eyes.

"Help her do some cleaning before y'all play anymore."

"What's the use? They'll clean and then wreck the same room."

"Ah, well, take it outside then, boys."

"It's raining here."

I'm pretty useless. It's frustrating when I'm so out of my element, especially with my own family. I hate these calls sometimes. I'm just a useless face on their screen. Even Sophia knows it. She tries to grab the phone, only to slam it on the table or hang up. Mary holds her distanced, so she wouldn't be able to. The boys impatiently wait at her side. They miss having me there, but they don't want to video chat; it interrupts too much fun.

"Ah, well, boys, don't make things too difficult for mom."

"How were the flights?" Mary asks.

I recant the flights and fictitious work I did. I don't mention the journal. She'd want to know what I wrote, but I don't share those things. Sophia starts crying, not wanting to be held any longer. She wants down to crawl after the boys. My daughter walks now, but to keep up with them, she has to use all fours. Otherwise, she'd stumble and trip, and they would be two rooms ahead of her.

"Mary, I'm going to let y'all go. I love you. I'll call later."

"Alright, love you." The call ends.

The small pizza shop is crammed with people, many wearing masks. They're wearing two masks these days, one to fake their happiness and the other to fake hygiene. After Covid, many people continued sporting small coverings over their faces. As if they weren't fornicating with strangers, trying new designer drugs, or eating nothing but slices of pizza every day.

"One slice of pepperoni."

"We're out, ten minutes before next ones ready."

I stand thinking, unsure what I'd like instead of waiting in this line for ten minutes. A line of hungry vultures waits impatiently behind me. They're all dressed in black, and each has on their sanitary face mask.

"One slice of cheese, then."

He hands it over as I pay, and I walk out with my slice. I consume the thing savoring much, I'm starving, and I'm getting tired of having a suitcase. I need to check in to my hotel. I need to research. I need to rent a car, and I need to find a priest.

*
**

I already miss my family. I miss the sound of my boys and them attacking me as I stand at the fridge. I miss Sophia hollering for me from her playpen. I miss Mary and her warmth. My hotel room is silent and small. There's a tightly made bed, but no wife in it. I lose a massive part of myself when I'm away from them. I never knew how much of me was them until I started traveling more. I'm hollow. They're an anchor for me; my mind runs wild without them around. Depression knocks at my door; I feel flat and two dimensional. Is this what it feels to be single? I wonder if people who haven't made themselves a family always feel this way. In modern culture, there's such a distaste for what I have at home. Do they know what I have at home? Do they comprehend the wonder of being handed finger paintings done by a one-year-old daughter with eyes observing your every move? Do they understand how it feels to be mimicked by boys aspiring to be like their father?

It would be best for me to stop traveling. I know it's true. It would be best for me to return home, call Tommy. It would be better if I didn't run around mysterious cities collecting dirt in my dustpan. It's a shame, but I need to do it. I can't quit. When I'm home, I have the opposite thoughts.

Mary sits sadly in her chair. She acts as if I can't see it, as if I don't know that it's there. I know when she's sad; always. It gets dreadful around the holidays, and she's been very low-spirited the past year. I see her enwrapped in her grief, and I immediately want to be out. I want to bring hell to all who have made such scars on precious things. There is no graver anger than what I have; there's no greater frustration than what I feel when I pretend I'm not taking note of its every effect on my wife.

The sick bastard died before I could get my hands on him. No one called his number. I guess the Angel of Death did, but that's not any good. Someone from this end of eternity should have had the chance. Someone should have been able to say, "I know what you are." He died five years ago, alone in his house, but on everyone's minds. He likely panicked, but not as everyone who suffered him did. For years they suffered and continue to suffer. He's unable to molest, but the memory of him is, and it does every day. It molests the woman who should be able to enjoy her little girl without fearing for her future.

"It's a girl." The ultrasound technician announced on a Monday morning in a beige exam room. The father was beyond excited; there was something magical about a little girl. The little person was something filled with love and joy. It made his heart warm just thinking of the little person who would do everything for him only by existing even if she never did anything.

The mother didn't rejoice. She was silent for a moment and began sniffling. Her eyes flooded with water, and soon after, her face was covered in streams of it. She didn't want someone to feel what she felt. She didn't want to worry about the little girl and all the nasty creatures that lurked outside.

"I'll give you two a minute." The technician stepped out.

"Mary," I said, "what's the matter?"

"She's safe now, but once she's born—"

Mary began to weep uncontrollably. I awkwardly tried to pet and comfort her. I looked for Kleenex and handed her the entire box.

"She'll have us, Mary. She'll have you. You know what's out there. We'll teach her how to be safe."

"There's no point. The wicked don't play by rules."

"I won't allow anything to happen to her. I promise."

She eventually stopped crying for a time. We left the hospital and went home. Later, I would find her weeping again soon after. I knew women are emotional when pregnant. I saw that with the boys, but she cried more. I would wake to hear her crying at night or early in the morning before the sun would rise. I heard her crying in the bathroom under the noises of the fan that she'd try to employ to mute the sound. She would cry and eventually stop crying, for a time, but she would cry again. She gained a lot of water weight while pregnant with Sophia, and I thought it was impossible because she wept so much. The boys had avoided her some in those days, and she'd begun crying about that too. It was months of misery, and I still had to travel for work. I felt such incredible guilt; I still feel guilt. That was when I began, in those days, that was when I started hunting. I struggled to justify my actions at first. The first one, the second one, the third, they were all difficult in their own ways. I dedicated, secretly, those first three to each of my children.

"When a man kills an evildoer, he is not a mankiller, but, if I may so put it, a killer of evil." I would see such quotes in the most bizarre places, *from saints*. Who could argue with the saints?

Sophia was born. I was in town for that; my bosses weren't so heartless to send me away at the birth of my first daughter. Mary was so strong. No one speaks enough of a woman in labor. People are always talking about how tough childless and career-focused women are as if doing something anyone is capable of is impressive. It isn't, but childbearing, labor, nurturing those first feeds at the breasts are. I always stand at the foot of her bed when she's pushing. I've continually watched as the crown of my children's heads enter our realm of existence. Every time, it's me that cuts the cord, like cutting the ribbon at a grand opening. My wife had been working tirelessly, creating this new human being, a person that had never existed before.

At labor, you see the final sweats and tears of her pregnancy; at least, that's how it is supposed to be. Mary would continue crying after Sophia, and I would continue hunting. I dedicated number four and all the ones that followed to the Kleenex boxes and runny mascara; I dedicated them to the times of night that Mary would wake.

*
**

Father Davis McKinney, the big fish, is just blocks away from me. I look out the window of my hotel, and I can see the very Church he is in. The grey-stoned steeples rise just enough past the trees to be seen, and the buildings that stand on either side of it aren't high enough to conceal it from me. It's raining. Everything is shiny and fresh when it rains; the water rinses the dust away. The only place dust remains is indoors, in homes and places where people work or live. All I have to do, really, is follow the dirt, follow the filth, and I will find the source of it all. I will find the heap of trash that is *Father* Davis McKinney. I will call his number, and he will answer. I will speak, and he will hear. I will cut, and he will bleed.

Tonight is the night I hope to find where he lives. Perhaps I'll be able to get invited in. I rented a car to trail him home. I'm hoping he goes home; I'm hoping he walks or rides home. There are so many points of failure. This part is the most stress-inducing, much more so than completing the act is. This is the hunt, the thrilling hunt.

Tomorrow, I have work. I'll have to pitch the deal to some men and women interested in devices that watch people die. If I'm not able to meet with him tonight, I'll have to try tomorrow night. The day after, I'll be preparing to go home, and I'll be ready if anything comes up last minute with either line of duty.

TEMPESTAS

Shhhhhhhhh-

The heavy rain mutes most other noises, and even the car horns are quieter under it all. The raindrops land individually on my umbrella, just as they all land separately elsewhere. You can hear each pop and drip, every tap, if only for a moment as they pelt the plastic covering. Our lives are just as short-lived as a droplet's. I look out and over the street and see rain falling, illuminated by nearby streetlamps and electronic billboards. So many trillions of individual droplets, and I'm sure God could name each of them; perhaps He has even placed them accordingly.

Any time I find myself in the rain, it makes me wonder; how many raindrops have fallen since the firmament broke? I read once that roughly one and a half trillion drops will make their journey down in a heavy rainstorm like this one. There's no math for the number of Mary's tears, and I'm sure with as much as she's cried, she hasn't surpassed even one heavy downpour, but a single teardrop from one of her eyes is worth more than a rainstorm. I watched the continuous rainfall, and I could see her tears that fell for months while she was pregnant and for months after. A streetlamp flickered and was off, and I could see her smiles fade from her face, replaced by frowns and emotionlessness.

I didn't speak to her after the incident. I was afraid to be chastised or have her make a scene. I didn't know what it was I had done, but I knew she was frightened by me. I only wanted her to get home safely, I cared for her, and I loved her. I was tempted to stop going to Mass for the following two or three weeks, but I continued. I sat by myself, on the other end of the church from her. I tried not to even look in her direction. It was the most challenging thing I had yet done in my life.

I bought my own Roman Missal, I learned the Mass for myself. I researched when I wasn't standing or kneeling beneath the martyrs and their marbled faces. I knew what the Mass was. I learned to think of it as a time machine, the very moment of the Crucifixion. I learned that Christ was the Eucharist, and I began to believe it. I studied the rosary. I didn't talk to Mary for months after the incident, but I spoke to the Blessed Mother. Her name was also Mary, but she didn't talk back to me, as far as I was aware, but that was okay. The Blessed Mother was always standing there, to my left. There were three altars in the church, one beneath the crucifix and massive mural of Christ, and two others that flanked both sides of Him. The church was laid out in a t-shape. On the left was the altar with Mary's statue, and on the right was Saint Joseph, the Terror of Demons.

I felt weird sitting on the left side, beside the Blessed Mother. All the elderly people sat there, some in wheelchairs, but I liked being near her. People often left flowers on her altar. I didn't know who did it, maybe it had been the priest or the cleaning ladies, but I had an idea to leave some of my own one Sunday.

I felt it fitting to buy the flowers on Mother's Day; I was a confirmed Catholic by then. I sincerely perceived her to be a mother of mine. I bought flowers for my mother as well, I got her sunflowers and posies, but for the Blessed Mother, I selected roses, of course. The bouquet came as a dozen, and Mary would have 12 roses to sit at her feet.

After visiting the store, I drove to Mass. The church parking lot was especially packed out, just as church parking lots are on all holidays. Holiday is Old English for Holy Day, and what's always been weird to me is that every Sunday is a Holy Day, really. Still, people pretend they don't have to go to church, but three times a year. I selfishly wish that only people that go to church weekly would go to church on the holidays, but I guess that's what penance is, not having it the way you want it.

The only available parking spot just so happened to be beside her car. My heart nearly jumped through my chest as I pulled in next to it.

I didn't want to look left, to her car, but I had to exit my vehicle. I was afraid she'd be looking back, but she wasn't even in the car. I must have been running a few minutes late because all the cars were empty.

I carried the roses in my hands. I brought the flowers for my mother as well; I didn't want them dying in the heat of my car. It was anxiety-inducing to carry them. I felt like a goober. I have always felt silly, holding flowers. Something is humiliating to it, but I reminded myself they were for the Blessed Mother, and I tried not to think in such a way.

I opened the large old wooden door, and the sound of Ave Maria being prayed by hundreds of people broke into the air. The Mass was packed out, about as full as it had been on Easter. The confession line in the back of the church was twenty people long, and I knew they wouldn't have a chance of making it all in time. You've got to be a lot quicker to reconcile with God than that. It's similar in life too, people wait to repent, and they don't always make it in time. The old women like to sit in the confessional for eons. I never knew what for. They don't do anything, but they've lived a lot. Perhaps they do a lot of reminiscing. I've read that the numbers are directly correlated with lifespan and worship attendance. Countries where people live fifty years do a lot better preparing for the afterlife than they do where people live to eighty.

I continued to carry both sets of flowers. I followed the leftward walls of the sanctuary until I came to her altar. She had already been visited by many. Some flowers were in vases with water. I felt dumb for not spending the extra ten dollars for a vase. My roses wouldn't last. I was sad about it, but I got over it. The Blessed Mother appreciated them, I'm sure. I knelt down before the statue that depicted the Holy Mother of God after placing my roses at her feet, and I prayed, asking for her intercession.

"Mother," I whispered very quietly, practically mouthing my words, "I beg you to ask Jesus Christ to heal whatever harm I caused. If it is His will, that she would be mine." I crossed myself, "In Nomine Patris, et Filii, et Spiritus Sancti. Amen." I stood with my mother's flowers and carried them with me to the place I had been sitting in the past couple of months. Mary was there, in my new usual spot, watching me. There's that feeling, like when you are being lifted up higher and higher along a rollercoaster. You know the drop will happen at any moment, that moment of terror, when your throat is unable to swallow.

I walked towards my seat, and she shuffled her things in the pew to make room for me, but really to show she didn't mind if I sat with her. Next to her, I sat down, pleased more than I have ever felt before in my life. Perhaps the roses were an excellent idea. When I sat with my birthmother's flowers, Mary leaned over to smell them as she continued to recite the prayers with the rest of the flock.

"Sancta Maria, Mater Dei, ora pro nobis peccatoribus, nunc et in hora mortis nostrae. Amen." I joined in, my Mary took notice of my newly learned Latin. Which was nice, but it wasn't anything compared to lining up for Holy Communion with her. We both knelt together, and by then, I knew what the bread was, the Body of Christ, and we both received our Lord together.

I prayed the same prayer from earlier, but I didn't ask for Mary's intercession with the Lord within me; I spoke silently to Him. I said inaudibly to God within me, to the Holy Sacrament that was within my own temple. I also asked that He help Mary with her sanctification, as He dwelt within her. Flesh of Christ, Bread of Life, heal us.

The Mass ended a short time after, and the two of us were able to talk. It was the moment I had been dying for. For months, all I had wanted to do is have a second chance with her, for her to learn that I wasn't a total creep. I wanted to display all that I had learned. I wanted, somehow, for advanced theological topics to casually come up in conversation or for her to ask me to pray something in Latin. It had to be a prayer in the rosary though, I hoped she wouldn't ask me to pray something off the wall, an ancient forgotten litany, or a supper prayer.

"It was very sweet of you to bring Mother roses. Very fitting."

"Shoulda brought a vase." I frowned.

"Maybe the priest will put them in one. I've seen him do that before."

"You think my mom will like these?" I asked, holding out the golden yellow sunflowers and posies. They matched the pink shade of Mary's nails, I noticed as she felt the petals. It sounds like such minute detail, but such things always stuck out to me. There's symbolism in everything, every color, and motion.

"I think so. They're different. People always buy the same darn flowers."

"Like roses?"

"Well, yes, but roses for our Mother is fitting. That's tradition, but buying flowers for your mother should be based more on what she likes or what makes you think of her. No flower says joy or happiness like the sunflower does. Most other flowers are the stuff you'd find at a funeral."

"That's exactly what I thought." Flowers were things of funerals. Flowers smelt like funerals; they looked like funerals. There should have been one flower used for funerals because all of them reminded us of death. Perhaps that's a good thing.

The sanctuary had emptied, and there were only a few stragglers on the other ends of the church, praying or cleaning. The Mother's Day folks vanished to attend their lunches. Mary's posture changed; she shifted in the pew. The smile on her face had tucked away.

"I wanted to apologize to you, Simon, for the night I snapped."

"There's no ne-"

"I know now that you were concerned."

"No, I'm sorry. I probably came off wrong. I didn't mean to alarm you and looking back, I probably sounded like a total creep. I promise I'm not."

"I know you're not. You gave me space and time to think. Creeps don't do that. Creeps don't stop." Her voice trembled.

I wanted her to keep chatting; I wasn't sure what to say. I was happy I wasn't blacklisted, but there was more to what she wanted to share, I didn't think she was finished, so I waited.

"And before that night, I found myself smitten. I liked having you near at Mass or in the cafeteria. It was nice having you around to help clean."

"Yeah?" I smiled. Smitten, was it just a cute word, or did she like me? It was all so childish in a way, but love is a childish thing.

"It's true, and then you kept coming to Mass, and you didn't sit with me or talk to me, and I missed it after I had calmed down."

"I missed it too."

"Then I saw you get confirmed. I saw you praying. I saw you this morning enter with flowers for Mother, and I think you're alright."

"I'm happy I passed your test." I laughed. I was happy to no longer be avoided, but I wanted to know. There was a deeper root, after all. There was something, something that would surely manifest again if I wasn't careful.

She looked over her phone's screen to check the time. I had neglected it was Mother's Day. To me, it had become Mary's Day, a day with both Mary's. I wouldn't tell my own mom about that, of course, but I sorta liked the idea of that holiday more. I didn't want to depart from Mary and the church, but I'm sure she had plans, and I did too.

"I've gotta do some last-minute shopping for my mom."

"Shopping on Sunday?" I shook my head, "tisk-tisk."

"Well, hypocrite," she laughed as she looked at the flowers in my hand, "I need to get my mom some frozen yogurt, and there's no way of keeping that secret."

"She's a woman of fine tastes, I see."

We both stood from our pew and walked to the doors. The sunlight burned through the fine cracks beneath the closed doors. My least favorite part was always leaving her or church, but especially now. She said she had been smitten with me, but I didn't want to be too forward in attempting anything. I was doomed to be friend-zoned, I supposed. My heart burned with a certain kind of sadness.

"We'll have to hangout sometime this week or maybe after Mass next weekend if things are too busy." She said.

"What? Hanging out? What about Ora et labora?"

"Ah, it'll be fine." She giggled. Our cars were parked next to each other, almost alone in the emptied parking lot. I felt nervous about walking in the same direction and driving out together. I didn't want her to get the wrong idea again.

"That's my car over there." I said, it was a silly warning of sorts. We made small talk on the walk. She didn't seem horribly uncomfortable and didn't snap. We departed from the parking lot and went our separate ways.

*
**

Shhhhhhhh

The rain continues to wash out all noises. It plays its song upon my roof. It's peaceful for once, or as peaceful as it could be. There are far fewer people walking along the streets. As for those who continue to be out and about, they endure silently to themselves. Each umbrella-wielding person is an island beneath the constant rainfall. Across the street, remaining in the rain, a schizoid, probably crying out about lab-grown babies and the rise of AI. The typical psychotic monologue, practically holding a conversation, but with no visible person taking part. It's tough to fully hear what he's saying from within the comfort of my car.

I continue driving as the light turns. The church isn't far, maybe one block further. The priest has been busy tonight holding his little meeting for the Fruits of Christ club; lately, he holds it every other night of the weekday. I know he's got about 30 minutes left and will then be finished. That will be the tricky part. I've failed at this point in the past. I'm very anxious I might fail again. It's infuriating to know the target, travel to them, and even see them, but to lose them in the mess of it all. Sometimes the dust doesn't easily collect when you sweep it. The dust flies off into the air and settles elsewhere, perhaps to be collected by someone else, possibly forgotten.

Before I enter the church, I do another check for all the items I need. Everything is tucked into one of the many pockets of my coat: the Ka-Bar, a box of gloves, additional masks, and clothes. I can't do anything without them.

THE SHRIVING PLACE

FRUCTUS CHRISTI

The church is gorgeous. It's far prettier than many built these days; the walls and glass are old and sturdy. They've survived much worse than a heretic, but they deserve better. They deserve to reflect the beauty of reprobates becoming holy. They deserve to shine with all the brilliance of Heaven, yet they are cursed to contrast with error. They remain standing beautifully still, against the false teachings, the abuse, the dirt, and crud of wickedness.

Father is laughing with his friends, his *Fruits of Christ*. It's a group of his personal flock, a truly lost group of individuals. It fills me with sorrow. I do not intend to be taken as someone who hates *them*. I really don't mind what a person *struggles* with. I've known plenty of same-sex attracted people, but the ones I've known well are ones who've put away those desires. They live chastely; even one I've spoken to has a family of his own. Such people could be saints.

These *Fruits of Christ* are called to live the same, yet they meet to talk and pray about the blessing of gay marriage as a Sacrament. They revel whenever the Pope seemingly speaks favorably on his hopes for the future. As for those who say we all deserve happiness, that is the idea of Heaven, perfection, and eternal bliss. It takes a sacrifice of our flesh in this life to hope for such a thing. I don't imagine people that seek such unashamed happiness in this life even believe in God. They believe in comfort and pleasant lies. Life is pain; glory is forever. This church, just as mine does, has saints all over it, perpetually pierced. Saint Bartholomew holds his own skin as he continues to point to Heaven. His marbled face is indifferent, although he experienced such pain. We should aspire for such sacrifice, yet many today are unwilling to stop the simplest of sins. They want to be pleasured. It's mostly their selfish natures, just as we all have, but a lot of it rests on *Father* McKinney's shoulders. It's priests like himself that contribute to this false hope. It's loud voices like his that attempt to control, to drown-out the truths that have been declared for thousands of years. When people pursue truth, when they seek Christ, they come wearing shackles to be freed. If there was a group for drug addicts, masturbators, fornicators, or alcoholics, it would be expected to find people congregating. Coming together in hopes of correcting their inclinations and learning not to act on them. Why must all other sinners reject themselves, yet some are encouraged to continue? He started this group that's no more than a speed-dating event, a

BRIAN PATRICK EDWARDS

meet-up for *Christ-loving* homosexuals. I wonder what will happen to the group when *Father* is no longer present at the events. They deserve to have companionship in their trials; they deserve to find communities that don't desire to burn them. They deserve a better leader, one that does not comfort them in their habits. You do not save a burning house by splashing gasoline on it.

One might say my action is misdirected. One may say I am doing a good thing, but I am fixated on the wrong people. I see no difference. A heretic and abuser are often one and the same. Even if they weren't, one makes the path for the other to stroll.

$$*\atop{**}$$

I spent more time with *her*. She warmed to me, she did like me, and she began to sincerely trust me over time. I showed no malicious plans. I loved her, I thought she was attractive, but sex was not my intent. I didn't desire to corrupt or to *trespass* on something that belonged to God. Yet, there was something sad in her, something anxiously chewing at her. I could see it occasionally. It took a great deal of patience at times to comfort her. There was a load of hurt in her heart, and eventually, she did confide in me. Mary resisted for so long, hoping not to disgust me. She did not want me to view her as a wilted flower. I wouldn't have and didn't.

"Simon." She said hesitantly. We were in an empty park on a Saturday, it was a beautiful day, but she didn't see it as I did.

"Yes?" I asked, thinking it was the end of our friendship. I was always a pessimist. She spoke in

56

a sort of break-up tone, although we weren't actually dating.

"Do you love me?" The words split my chest open. I looked into her eyes with my heart pounding and my face heavy and numb. I feared my face was turning red, hoping not to reveal the wrong things.

"I do love you." I said, the first time I uttered the words. I was frightened by what would come of it. I didn't want her to leave my life if she hadn't felt the same, but I dove in.

"In what way?"

"In all ways. Maybe I was just fascinated by you at the start, but I love you almost as much as I love the Mass."

"Is there anything that would make you love me less?" She spoke in the language of sadness, leading somewhere darker. I wasn't sure where that would go.

"I don't think so. Is something the matter?" I picked up the fallen orange leaf that was next to me on the park bench. She turned towards me and held her hand out for the leaf, and I passed it to her. It cracked and crunched between her fingers.

"Remember the night in the parking lot?"

"Yes."

"It had nothing to do with you. It wasn't your fault. I know now that you were just being a gentleman."

"I know."

She was quiet for a moment, but I could sense the tide coming in. She had more to say as she nervously picked and tore at the once beautifully intact orange leaf.

"I've had similar struggles for a few years now. Sometimes I get scared, I panic, I get defensive. I push people away; I just don't want to push you away."

"It would take a whole lot more than that to get rid of me."

"I thought I had pushed you away that night. You didn't talk to me for the longest time."

"I wasn't pushed away. I was giving you space. I hoped every Sunday to get a chance to talk to you."

"I know that now, but it's still a worry I have."

"No need to worry."

"Several years ago-" She looked at the leaf, its edges crumbled away, most of what remained was the stem and dried veins, "-I was molested many times."

"That's awful, Mary. I am so sorry." There was nothing I could say.

"It was a priest, and I was an altar-girl. I've just always had problems of sorts since. It's got nothing to do with you—I struggle with that sometimes. It gets worse around this time of year."

"How old were you?"

"Twelve. I didn't say anything about it for the longest time either. I just held it in silently, mostly anyway. My mother was so worried, I would throw such fits about having to go to Mass there. I couldn't stand going to that church. She didn't know what had happened; she said later that she assumed I was just going through a rebellious phase. Everyone else seemed to love that priest. They all thought he was a really *good one* until he abused some kids that became more vocal than I was. I could have been the one to prevent others-" she stopped briefly and went along, "someone told their parents, and suddenly the entire place erupted in accusations. It's insane what things happen beneath our very eyes; horrible things are always being done all around us. I learned that. I learned that this world really wasn't a fantastic place to be and that there are monsters out there. I was just a child. Before, it all had magic in it, how exhilarating holidays were, the wonder of being a child. I was woken from that. The world is cold and bitter."

"What happened to the priest?"

"They relocated him across the country, out of the ministry, I think. I was never told exactly where, maybe the Midwest. He's dead now. He was pretty old, to begin with. Many people thought it was his age that affected him, but some older abuses came up. Things he did years beforehand."

"Geez, Mary, that's freaking horrible." I shook my head in disbelief. I couldn't imagine that the worst of crimes were unpunished. At that moment, I thought of all the other criminals that sat behind bars or waited their days out on death row, yet the worst of them seemed to be punished with nothing more than retirement.

"How are you even able to go to Mass?" She was clearly stronger than I could dream of being. I hadn't experienced much, "I feel like I would have lost the faith entirely."

"I don't know, I guess I figured that many saints were priests, so not all priests were *demons*. A part of me felt that a more traditional church would be better. Perhaps finding a priest that truly feared God would help. Realized that it wasn't God that did it. I need Him. I needed His healing, His graces. So, I convinced my mother to take me to Blessed Sacrament. We went there for the longest time, even though she wasn't a fan of the Latin Mass. She would drive me every Sunday until I was able to take myself."

She told me later, just before we left the park, that she did *love* me. She loved me as I loved her. It was what I had craved to hear; it was the *only* thing I had wanted to hear. I didn't want to learn that she had suffered so much. Of course, not because I didn't care, but because I cared so much. I didn't think of her returned love that night; I thought of the children in the world robbed of innocence.

*
**

It was shocking. All things are shocking, but this, in particular, morphed into an obsessive series of thoughts I've had since. She was driven to Blessed Sacrament because of all that had happened to her. Had she never been abused, or had she not continued her Mass attendance, would I have ever met her? Would I have become Catholic? Even to this day, I'm haunted, along with the joys in my life. I'm proud to wrestle with my boys and feed Sophia a spoon full of mashed fruits. Still, Mary's scars are always visible, even when they're not so noticeable on the surface.

And *Father* McKinney is leaving. His disgusting gathering has departed the church, and I will not lose him. I have him. He is just before me in the rain, with his umbrella, keeping all the dirt that he is from becoming mud. He enters the church parking lot. I can smell his cologne as it lingers just behind him. It is the same as the scent of flowers at funerals, a thin mask to hide the decay within.

He will pay for what's been done. I will hear his truth, the truth as it is to him. I will listen to all he has to say, and I will tear away all that he is. I will pull the curtain back. My actions will be the precursor to his final judgment that waits just beyond this delicately veiled life of ours. I will surrender him lifeless to the Godhead, and he will be cast into Hell for all eternity with the rest of them. He will be cursed by the poor souls he led there. He will be cursed and stomped by the demons in Hell, the fiends will be disgusted with him and his degeneracy. I will be the Forerunner of Judgement, the Forebear of Lamentations.

I quickly jump into my rented Honda, start the engine, and I keep my eyes fixed on him as he unlocks his own, a Prius. His platinum toupee remained dry beneath the umbrella. He closes it awkwardly as he tries to get in without getting too wet. I wonder if he is impatient to get home, impatient to die. It's funny to think that we just want to skip forward so many times in our lives. Oh, how we would love to enjoy our time standing in the rain if we knew the sands in our hourglasses were almost drained. I steer towards his every direction.

I check for my *mask; I* bought a special one for the upcoming occasion. It's among the most important of my tools. It's in my coat, along with my Ka-Bar. Confidence and façade go a long way, but the same is not true for *Father* Davis McKinney, at least not any longer. It's been true for him for years. His entire career, even, but it has damned him. Tonight, he will find the truth of his spinning of lies. He's the spider that dies in its own web, a carcass wrapped in its own traps.

He's on his phone, we're stopped at another light. I am close enough, I can see clearly into his car. The color of his screen shows a deep blue. I know what app he's using. He's using that app that gave him a blue checkmark, the app that has no problem with false information when it pertains to heresy. Post something about an election or some hurtful statistics, you'll get blurred out or deleted. Post something contrary to Catholic teaching, call it Catholic, and they will broadcast you everywhere. I check my own phone to see what exactly he's doing. I need to know if he is planning something. I'm hoping he's going home, but I'm not optimistic. We could be going anywhere for all I know. This is an arduous job; it's more disappointing than not.

In the reflection of my rearview, I see driving behind me a familiar shaggy man. The man from the plane? I spin my head immediately, to see nothing of the sort. Instead, I see two Asians sitting, staring blankly into the air. One looks up at a billboard, uninterested. Bizarre. Perhaps I'm getting anxious. I do a double-check of my neighboring cars. There is no shaggy man in any of them. I return my attention back to the phone, back to the app that *Father* loves so much.

Had a great turnout tonight at Fruits of Christ. We talked about famous quotes in the Bible and how many passages that are believed to be about homosexuality are condemning pedophilia.

He shares an article along with his message, a website known for biblical revisionism. I'm not impressed; it's all trash. This same site questions the divinity of Christ. Anyone with a functioning brain could see it for what it is, but people like to sin. People want to be *free*, and modern Catholics don't wanna be rigid on their loved ones. They don't want to give up their comfortable friendships. They don't want to pray for someone's conversion of heart. They would like to accept the fact that God *made* them this way, that it's all *love.*

Father doesn't have any plans other than going home. This is good. This is very good. Perhaps I'll be able to accomplish tonight's mission. Hopefully, no one lives with him. Hopefully, he does not have visitors. I don't think he is; that all goes against his continued social distancing M.O.

His car slows and pulls into a driveway just off the main street. I watch his vehicle through my rearview mirror. He drives forward into the narrow garage. Fortunately, it's still raining as well. Rain makes trailing a little easier to blend in. Rain drowns out noise; it helps to keep me under the radar.

CAPTUS

Water streams over the outside of my windows. I imagine Sophia cozily zipped into her sleep-sack, and her mouth hanging open, drooling as she dreams about chasing after her brothers. I picture my sons asleep in their messy rooms and the silence in those rooms after a long day of being loud and rowdy. Mary has likely already dozed off as well. She works so hard on the cleanliness of our home, on the quality of our children. I miss them much, but I must put such things out of my mind.

It's hard at times to keep my mind from drifting back to my little family. I need to keep focused on the spider in his web. I need to keep my eyes fixed on his house, watching, waiting. I'm wondering if it's safe now, safe to strike. I'm wondering if someone, a friend maybe, or possibly a Fruit of Christ will show up at his house. I'm hoping, praying, that he will have no other visitors tonight, no visitors aside from myself.

I reach into my coat pocket and probe for the mask I've brought. My fingers touch the metal, wood, and leather of my sheathed Ka-Bar, no not yet. In the deep pockets, I feel around. I find its soft cloth and the strings that wrap around my ears. I pull it out of my coat; it's striped, blue, pink, and white in the center. *TRANS LIVES MATTER* is written across the center. I picked it, specifically, for my encounter with this priest. It's one of the benefits of this post-pandemic world. You can conceal your identity, even cover it with lies, and without saying a word to do it. I hide my identity from cameras and people alike, all while appearing to only value our overlords' professional opinions. To them, my mask is a blessed sight, a welcomed one. I also have a beanie to wear, just a normal black one. I use it to cover my ears. Supposedly, your ears have *prints* just like your fingers do. Everyone's ear is shaped differently, and this has been used many times to catch the suspects who only thought to wear a mask. It would be nice to wear a hoodie, but I haven't got one that has enough pocket space.

I have my gloves ready as well, but they're not covering my hands yet. They're non-latex. Latex isn't good enough. Some say they're thin enough to leave fingerprints, so I use Nitrile gloves. They're thicker but can cause allergic reactions. I've never had a reaction wearing them, but I'm always interested in triggering a *Bad One* to have one. I'm not positive how severe the result would be, probably a lot less severe than a stab from a Ka-Bar. I laugh. *No one* actually wore gloves during the pandemic. They're still a bit suspicious to people. I'll wait to put them on once I'm ready to make a move. I must be sure not to touch *anything* until that moment.

I think of my woman at home, Mary, the most beautiful. She shouldn't be alone, I know that. I should be there. I'm tired of her tears. I'll be there to wipe them away for the remainder of our lives. For now, I'm going to bring some balance to this disgusting nation we live in. Evil is celebrated and protected, and the people of God weep in their homes.

Amen, Amen I say to you, that you shall lament and weep, but the world shall rejoice; and you shall be made sorrowful, but your sorrow shall be turned to joy.

I don't call their numbers without them answering. I've asked them questions, always ask the questions, and find others in need of detachment from the world. I sweep, collect the dust and dirt, and I see more dirt. A clean floor sparkles and reveals the filth elsewhere. I go to the grime, I clean, and by the time I'm finished there, it's as if someone's walked through the door with muddy shoes. The cleaning never stops. My wife has wept for long enough. She's shaken in the night and sighed one million times, and I've never been able to heal her. It won't go without correction. None of them will go without punishment. *Father Davis* is guilty. A priest confessed it to me as his number was called. My sorrow will be turned to joy tonight.

When the wicked perish, there are shouts of joy.

He lives in a finer neighborhood. The houses are bricked here; they're older but not unkempt. I keep watch of the house he entered. The windows of the house are still black with no light from within. I believe that it's safe to say that no others are present, only the priest. Hopefully there's no dog. The blinds are down in his house, and they're undamaged. Damaged blinds equal a dog, and so it's also safe to assume there's no four-legged friend in his home. Bad mistake on his part, but it's been said that animals don't like *them*. Imagine living your entire life alone because not even house pets enjoy your company.

I can see, from this angle, lights coming on from within the bricked home. The rain that passes just before the lights glimmer and returns to darkness as it falls. Only for a brief moment are they honest, not by their own choice, but by the existence and effect of the light. Only for a moment have they revealed themselves, soon to be ended upon impact, joined with the water and earth. It's a lot like tonight, and the wolf in sheep's clothing revealed and made honest by the fear of death.

I approach the front door. I'm only a lost man in the wrong neighborhood, with no one to call for help, because my phone is *dead.* It isn't, I've only turned it off, and I'm sure to keep track of it tonight. It will not wander from my pocket.

I knock on the door; the doorbell is broken. I'm thankful it isn't one of those surveillance doorbells. I had one of those once. I saw its glowing blue circle from the street and avoided being seen on it. I entered another way. Tonight, however, there is no camera, and I'm increasingly thankful. Keeping things simple.

I hear his footsteps approaching behind the door. There are glass windows on both sides of the door, with curtains covering them, but he draws one back and peers through to see who's at his door. He's a mouse, poking from his hole, and I am the cat with my claws ready but hidden.

I calmly wave to him. I can't afford to look like a psycho. I can't afford to look like anything other than a typical man lost on a random street of the infinite maze of Long Island neighborhoods. He moves away from the window, and I hear the door unlock.

Clunk

"Hello?" He asks in his typical soft tone. Typical it is because I've heard it so many times. His effeminate voice carries across the radio waves to distant lands. Many listen to this voice. Many know this voice. These are the soft tones that lure them all into the pits of Hell. His speech is like the music of the Pied Piper, but it won't be played again, not after tonight. Perhaps some will continue hearing recordings of it, talking about the hope of gay unions or the beauty of child transgenderism. Still, there will never be new words, never new sounds.

"Hey, sorry to bother you at such an hour." I pull my phone out to show him the black screen. "I'm here in Merrick visiting a friend, and I wrote the wrong address down before I went out to the city. My phone died and my taxi already left. Would you mind letting me use a phone to call my friend?"

The priest looks hesitant. He looks me over with his beady eyes. It's bizarre to know you're being judged by such a person. It's strange, wondering what impressions he has of me. In his mind, *I'm* the one that can't be trusted. What audacity to judge, knowing that you're the worst of monsters. It is survival, even if that's all his judgment is. He's a predator in a jungle. I can see his eyes detect the words written on my mask. There's a spark of excitement in his face.

"What's your name?" There's a change in his face. He loosens up on his silent inquisition. His eyebrows are no longer scrupulously squinched, but his eyes are just as soulless as ever.

"I'm Simon."

"Nice to meet you, Simon. I'm Davis." He opens his door wider to welcome me in. It's neat within. From what I can see, his home is tidy and remarkably polished. I follow his lead and step inside his home. It's his lair. Monsters don't have homes; they have lairs. They have dungeons, caves, *dwellings*, but they never have *homes*. Homes are for humans; he's no human. He is something diabolical manifested in the flesh. Nothing more. He closes the door once I'm through.

"Thanks, Davis. I really appreciate it." I reply as I look upon his walls.

There's modern art everywhere. Modern Jesus, painted in hippy-style, with ugly colors and distorted shapes. Why did anyone ever desire to do something other than baroque or byzantine is beyond me. It's like we ascended to the peak of a mountain, the pinnacle of art, and tucked our legs and rolled away immediately. His art isn't entirely religious in nature. There are bizarre statues and paintings as well. There are paintings of children with monstrous faces, holding balloons, and hands with beasts. I have no time to take note of it all. I must not get distracted. I can look *later*. We enter his living room briefly to pass through and into his kitchen, where the phone hangs on a wall.

His back is still turned to me. I can't use the phone. I don't know anyone's number, and if I called any numbers I knew, I'd incriminate myself. How nice of you, *Father*, but you shouldn't let people into your homes. They might know you're a pedophile and attempt to kill you. The only *number* I will call is *yours*.

I already have my gloves on.

"Hey, *Father-*" I say as he reaches for the phone on the wall; he turns around. The confusion on his face is palpable and immediately rinsed away by the upward blow of my fist to the bottom of his chin. He drops.

I had to really work on my form. I had started my *business trips* with brass knuckles. I broke too many jaws with them. Makes my investigations impossible, so I had to put them away. He's out cold, but his jaw isn't broken. I'm not going to have to decipher his slurred words. That wouldn't have been fun. I was never able to get better at interpreting the noises from a broken jaw. I drag his body from the kitchen to the living room. The time people spend knocked out varies, but he's about as down as they get.

There is a nice chair in here that I can place him in. I hoist his body onto it. Just the touch of him grosses me out, like picking up a cockroach or a maggot covered rat corpse. I can't help but laugh with glee at the sight of his drooping face. How I've waited for this moment. Really, he's the cherry on top of my mound of pedophiles and heretics. I've killed others, yes, and it was terrific, but he was just so much more enticing. He's a celebrity of sorts, a *man* with a massive following. This is big-game hunting.

I pull out my trusty Ka-Bar and duct tape. I tape his wrists together. I crisscross over and under his hands a couple of times. I tape over his fingers, making them impossible for him to use, impossible for him to tear away with. I wrap up his feet in a similar way. I tape his legs together, just above the knee; the tape runs low. I unplug his lamp, and then I cut the cable at the base of the fixture. It's long enough. I only need a few, and he doesn't need his cords. The dead don't require lights, they don't need TVs, they have no use for cooking appliances or *telephones*. That phone cable would be perfect; I don't even need to cut it. I'll unlatch it. I tie the-- is he breathing? Yes, he's breathing, only asleep. He's been out a lot longer than most would be. I tie him to the chair. I use the phone cable to tie him down to the chair I've placed him in. I weave it through his arms and over his chest and then over the backside of the chair, tightly. I test it, the cable is firmly placed. It's really all to prevent him from running or getting away fast enough. I have a

knife. I'll be within reach of him the entire time.
He won't go anywhere, and if he tries, well—.

INQUISITIO

I search his cabinet for some ammonia, yes, just where it ought to be. I take a glass and pour a fair bit of salt in it. I wonder if it's exorcised. This priest? No chance. He likely doesn't believe in demons, which I find remarkable, considering he practically is *one*. I look over the bright grains of white magnificence at the bottom of the cup. I pour a bit of ammonia in it. The smell is absolutely repulsive, in the strongest sense. It doesn't *stink*, but it's overpowering. It burns the nostrils and will put any mind on red alert at first scent.

I walk back to the living room, to the tied priest, a groan resonating from him. I will use my concoction anyway because I need him wide awake. I have a rag to stuff in his mouth if he shouts too much. I lean down, hold the glass out under his nose, and watch as his head jerks away from it. He coughs violently. His eyes are wide open.

"Ah-!" He screams, so I stuff the rag in his mouth. He continues to shout, mutedly, in pain as the rag puts pressure against his jaw. After a few moments of his whining, he begins to cry and whimper, defeatedly.

When I was a child, I'd see my cat toying with some vermin. The injured animal would stagger around with a missing leg, and the cat would slap at him and slap at his tail. It wasn't a simple kill. It never was; it was always with sport involved. The cat would break the little creature's spirits so that the miserable thing would no longer run. It would accept its death, willingly.

"Father Davis, I'm going to need you to promise me that you won't be screaming like that anymore, alright?" I look at his face, but he refuses to make eye-contact. "Father Davis? You're all tied up, and your neighbors can't hear you. It's raining again outside. They're all glued to their shows and movies." He doesn't respond. "I need you to nod if you agree. I need to discuss some things with you."

He finally gives in and nods his head. His glasses hang crookedly off his face; I adjust them for him and then remove the rag. He screams for help. Of course, I would too if I were in his place. I shove the rag quickly back into his mouth. It's annoying to me. If he knew my plans for him, which he's probably assumed already, he should know that there is no escape. It's all tiresome. I place the concoction on a nearby end table.

"Father Davis, if you insist on screaming after I remove this rag-- and sir-- this is your final warning, I will cut away bits of you as punishment. Please don't scream. I don't wanna make any more of a mess than I have to." The terror is plain across his face. It's a strange sight to see, a grown man in such fear. He nods again, tears streaming from his face, just as tears flow from Mary's, but they aren't the same. His tears are not worth a rainstorm. They aren't worth anything.

"What—what do you want from me? Are you going to kill me?" His voice is different. It isn't the voice I hear on his heretical videos. It's not so soft and confident; it's edgy and defeated.

"I'm not going to kill you." I lie. I do not need hysterics. I need answers.

"You're going to kill me." He whimpers pathetically.

"I'm not."

"Why else would I—would I be tied up like this?"

"Because I need you to answer these questions. No running away, no avoiding, just face-to-face honesty."

"Okay." He isn't convinced, but to go along with the inquisition is all he has.

"Do you remember Father Gulli?" I know they were friends. He looks at me blankly. He knows. "He was the priest a couple years ago that made a big mess with his altar boys, remember?"

"Yes, of course, I remember."

"That's not surprising to me, considering you're the one that helped with his case."

"I don't understand." He tries to shift into a more comfortable position. He isn't going to find one. "What is it you want? If he did something to you, you'd need to contact the Diocese."

"No, no, I don't want *their* money."

"Then what is it?"

It's incredible to me, perhaps capitalism is partially to blame, that such grave offenses can be met with monetary restitution. How could anyone dare think that Mary's pain or those altar boys' traumas are satisfied by dollars? Oh, you've been permanently scarred? Have you been made miserable? Here's a hundred-thousand dollars; enjoy paying for your lawyers and treatments. Absurd, for anyone who could imagine that it would be sufficient, that it would be just.

"I want to know why you made his life comfortable. Why did he deserve protection?"

"It was a mercy."

Punishment, that is the justice for the unjust.

"Why give mercy when justice is demanded?" It is more merciful to give justice to the community than to an individual undeserving of it. He was a grimy, revolting worm. His last moments should have been an act of mercy for all spectators. It's a shame it had to be done privately, in secret, by my own hands.

"Father Gulli's sexuality isn't his fault. He was born that way. God *made* him that way. How could we judge him for it?"

"You knew of his *past*? You knew of his previous abuses? He had been relocated after some short time in *rehab*. It's strange, unbelievable that you could rationalize defending such a stain on society."

"We were trying to protect the image of the Church." He admits, almost as if that's something worth keeping secret.

"Protect the Church!" I laugh, not humored by his words, but the sheer absurdity to it. "The Church looks best when it doesn't free Barabbas. How could you think for a moment that protecting abusers, re-abusers is a good look for Holy Mother Church?"

He cries.

"Are you a homosexual, Father?" He is uncomfortable with the question, where is his *pride*? Isn't he about taking pride in such inclinations?

"No," he says and begins moving his jaw, testing the soreness, wincing in pain as he does so.

"You aren't attracted to men?" I watch his eyes; I watch for lies.

"I am."

"But you're not a homosexual?"

"I find beauty in *everyone*."

I disregard his answer for now. I'm working my way into his mind, taking what avenues I need to. I need to know. I need to understand why.

"And what about Father Gulli? Were you two ever romantically involved?"

"No. He didn't like me in that way."

"Why not?"

"*Clearly*, he liked younger people."

"Younger?"

"He was a Hebephile." He speaks in terms, words, new words for old things we already have descriptors for. He was a sexual predator. "He was drawn to young teenage boys."

"The teenage boys he abused, against their will? The teenage boys he performed his sadomasochism on?"

He doesn't say anything. The bound priest knows that I've done my research. He, likely, assumes I'm the one that carved up his friend months ago. He takes a moment to think over his next word. "Yes."

"The only logical explanation, one that explains why you knew what he *was* and continued to protect him after what he had *done*, is that you, yourself are the same."

The priest begins to sob and breathe over the sobs, almost hyperventilating. It's infuriating to hear the crying. They always cry. Most do, at least. There are some truly detached people in the world, but these past few have been so emotional. They become hysterical and find it difficult to answer my questions. I had wanted to buy *truth serum* for such times, but the shelf life for Barbiturates is impossible to work with. I must be patient. Eventually, the crying will stop. He will regain his composure.

I look about the room as he continues to weep. His living room is just as sad. The art isn't awe-inspiring, the furniture is ugly, and his home is empty of family photos. Is a monster made miserable, or does the misery make the monster? It's hard to say, and perhaps it's not the right question. I'm sure that it's a bit of both. Why does modernity call for us to excuse the monsters? All of these new movies are apologetics for the classic villains. It's no wonder people are no longer up in arms about sexual deviants. The masses have been blindfolded by *good intentions* and illogical *sympathy*. The priest becomes quiet.

"Am I going to die?"

"*Father*, I'm just asking you some questions, that's all."

"What else do you want?" He sniffles.

"What is your argument for such inclinations?"

"Regarding what? The hebephilia?"

"Sure."

"Well, my great-grandmother," His voice is weary. He anxiously looks for words. He's on the edge of a cliff, and he's thinking like it, "was married and impregnated at the age of fourteen. That was *normal* then." He's given this a lot of thought. The words spit out faster as he finds his *monologue*. "They said she still played with dolls when she was married away. Would you say that my great-grandfather was wicked? Were all of our ancestors wicked?"

"*Father* Gulli liked young boys. He tortured them!" I snap a bit. My emotion gets the best of me. Settle down, Simon. "He, in no way, is the same as our ancestors. Our ancestors *had* to start early. It wasn't a fetish of theirs. They needed to build a family before time took its toll."

"Well, you would think, but for the homosexual, often it's an older counterpart that helps younger people discover their sexual identity."

"It *that* what happened to you?"

"Yes."

"And you figured you'd perpetuate this system? You never dared to fix it?"

No response, aside from his crying.

"That's disgusting!" I can't help my outburst. It's shocking to hear such things, and even more so for someone to *say* such things. "That's grooming. These boys were taken to the beach on a so-called retreat, only to be attacked by some old pervert!"

"Who's to say there's no love involved, to some extent?"

"Your great-grandmother was taken in by her husband for life. She was his duty. Your friend, on the other hand, was vile trash that took advantage of *children*. He was a rapist."

"Not all of the boys *were* straight."

"It doesn't matter. A priest, a supposed Man of God sexually abused *children!*" I shout. I'm beyond angry with this *priest* and his audacity. He is so accustomed to speaking to his fellow folk that he forgets reality. The priest is quietly terrified. He secludes himself as much as he can beneath his bindings. He makes very little noise.

"You believe yourself to be a pioneer on new frontiers of sexuality. You consider yourself a Doctor of the Church in the modern age, don't you?" It's almost enough to make me laugh, but it isn't funny. It's not a skit; it's real.

"The Fruits of Christ need love and community."

"Whatever happened to suffering with Christ?"

"I'm suffering with Christ right now, just as He did on the pillar."

I shove the rag into his mouth tightly. He fidgets and gags. I bring out my knife that I've had placed away. I get closer to the bound man. He eyes the black-bladed knife and squints his eyes as tears plummet from them. I reach behind him, to his bound hands and stick the steel into the small space between his fingernail and skin, and slowly twist and turn the tip of the blade. The finger becomes red with blood and drips out onto the oriental rug as his screams are muffled by the rag and his movements restrained by the power cables and duct tape. I lean back up, facing him directly.

"Don't for a moment, compare yourself to Christ on the pillar. He was spotless. He was an innocent prisoner; you are not. You don't know the first thing about suffering. You have your temptations as we all do. To deny them is not really suffering. To be raped, to love someone who has been raped, that is to suffer. My wife is a survivor of a *monster* similar to you and your friends. I've had to endure suffering with her because *that* is what love is. Love is suffering; love is not the pleasing of temptations."

I think of her while he writhes in his earned fear and pain. It's a bit of liberation to hear him. I think of her and all we've been through in our marriage. It's justice. It's almost perfect justice. Oh, how I wish I could do this publicly for all of those, now grown, children to see that their pain wasn't forgotten or hidden away. It's a total shame. The thunder blasts outside his house. The storm still rages on, and the priest continues to fight against his inescapable destiny. His drool drenches the cloth; saliva pulls at the fabric as the rag is removed from his mouth.

"You're going to kill me. I'm going to die. Oh, Lord, have mercy on me." He cries.

"Do you actually believe?"

"In what?" He asks, his voice is hoarse and dry. These are the priceless sounds I've always wanted to hear. I've watched him *proudly* displaying all of his sacrileges online and in lectures. It's a sweet victory, just to perceive the hopelessness in his speech.

"I want to know whether or not you believe in God."

"Yes, I do."

"You believe He would have mercy on you?" I would laugh again, but I keep the humor to myself.

"It's a sin to despair. All I can do is hope."

"What about that article you wrote about Hell being symbolic?"

"I don't know." He stops stuttering through his tears so much, "You would call it wishful thinking, but nothing wrong with hope." He sniffles.

"No, hope is good, but too much of it, and it becomes something else entirely." I clean the blood off my knife with his rag. If I need to use it again, it would be nice if he tasted his own bitterness. "I hope for my sake that God has mercy on you. If the Father forgave such a wretched beast, there's even more hope for the rest of us. But, we can't *live* like that, now can we?"

He likely clings to such silly ideas, that Hell is symbolic, because he cannot perceive what true justice is. Heaven and Hell are the Just Rewards. Of course, Hell isn't in his vocabulary properly because he creates such injustice in this life. His entire system is broken. It would be easier to describe law to an ape.

The priest doesn't answer. He knows the odds are stacked against him. Frankly, his only hope, really, is that religion is all a myth. It would be nice for him if death was black and empty, like sleeping, but without the dreams. Perhaps God's Mercy would save him, and perhaps only. It's a great question. What's next for this *priest*?

Heaven? A reunion with child molesters?

Hell? A reunion with child molesters?

Purgatory? A reunion with child molesters?

Something other, entirely?

I *hope* not. I hope they all *live* forever in shared suffering. I hope they suffer what they've made others suffer. I want eternal torment for them.

"Say, *Father*, I know what might help you before the Almighty." It probably won't, but it's always worth a try. He's a treacherous *one*, but they're the only ones I feel comfortable with.

"What? What is it?" He seems almost hopeful. He's eagerly pecking at the crumps of chance like a starved rodent. His crumbs of a chance to him are the salvation from my bindings and imminent threat. Really, his only hope is that God grabs him before falling into Hell. I have no intention of leaving him breathing. He would be a fool if he thought it possible.

"If you listen to my confession."

"You want *me* to hear your confession?" The bound priest asks. The electrical cables tied around him are the closest thing to a stole he has. It doesn't matter; the mark of the priesthood is eternally on him. He doesn't need the garments.

"You're a *priest*." He looks downward, closes his eyes, and seems to wait for me to continue with those sacred humble words, the words that are a life raft to all lost souls. He certainly wishes for the same. They're not always so helpful. I've had priests reject me outright. I heard nothing but blood-curdling screeching until the moment they were empty and returned to dust, collected and disposed of.

"Go on."

"Father," I really try to mean the words, the timeless words, "forgive me, for I have sinned. It's been-" When had Father Gulli expired? Six months ago? "It's been six months since my last confession."

LUCTUS

Drip—drip-drip

I think of all I've done. I'm no saint. Clearly, I'm no saint. I'm a murderer, don't you forget. Some would call me a saint, just because I'm the garbage man of this filthy world we call home. I'm not even that. I'm an obstinate sinner in need of a savior like all others. I'm a lustful man; God should have made the men without eyes, but no one could trust a woman then. Then again, Samson had eyes, for a time.

I'm a horrible husband and father. I truly am. I have this bloodlust, this mission to kill. I don't know what God thinks of it all. I've never been blessed enough to speak to Him. He said blessed are those who believe without seeing. My eyes are sore, Lord. I'd much rather be the least blessed and see Your glory early. I need answers, guidance because I am lost.

I'm a horrible son, I never visit my parents or grandparents, forgive me, Blessed Mary. I am the worst of your slaves, I know. I always thought, being her worst slave would make me her primary focus, but I don't deserve the Queen of Heaven on my shoulder. I don't deserve any of it, and it's a mystery why God has blessed me so. Perhaps, the pain and guilt I feel, being so blessed, is His punishment on me, knowing what I would be. But why punish my family?

Indeed, there is a way out of this abyss. I truly hate these priests. I try not to, even as I kill them, I truly hate them, but it's seemingly impossible. I should go home. I should go home and call Tommy. How I wish for the chance to return to my little Sophia, clean of homicide, and unpolluted with the intent to kill. How I yearn to be the father that she would need in times to come. I would protect her from all of her pot-smoking friends, teach her that she's beautiful because she wouldn't know it. They never know that they are beautiful. They find themselves ugly, but I would make sure she knew just how much God blessed her. She and those beautiful blue eyes, the curls, that smile that melts hearts. I can't stand to think she may one day be without a father like her mother was, and then what would be the point of any of this?

What the hell have I been doing? Why have I been sent on this path? Pater Noster, I've prayed one million times. Lead us not unto temptation. Oh, what a world we live in, where the unjust thing to do is most righteous, and the just things are covered in the collateral sin of tolerance and unmerited empathy.

"Father," I become emotional. I may have begun tearing at the edges of my eyes. Oh, how wonderful it feels to be moved to tears. I ache for it. Honestly, I do. I ache for the cold liquid on my cheeks as my sorrow pours forth.

The priest squirms in his bindings. It is quite awkward, really. I'm trying to have a heartfelt moment, and his noise is distracting me.

"I'm a wretched sinner, father. I've gravely sinned." I continue with all of the standard sins of a man. I cover the recent transgressions, things that have stuck out, all that I've meditated on. I think hard, hard as I can about the past six months, and really, it's not all so spotless, not as immaculate as the fogginess of my own mind. I know for a fact that there are tens of thousands of sins lying beneath that same fog. Yet, I draw a blank; I simply cannot tolerate the idea of being just as damned as these Bad Ones I've put away, "I uh-"

"Have you broken any laws?" He asks after I've been silently thinking for some time. I'm not sure how long I thought for, but I'm slightly irritated by his question. Of course, I've been violent.

"Yes, father. I've been very violent." It does still rip at me, to know the things I've done. It's hard to hold my children at times, but I often remind myself I do it for them. The priest begins crying again, trying to remain as quiet as possible. I can still hear him.

"Perhaps—maybe talk about that in more detail?"

"What?" I shout, "what do you want me to say?"

He says nothing.

"Should I start with my wife?" The sadness I've felt moves to anger. I no longer want to cry, but make another cry instead. "How she seemingly escaped the scars men like yourself left on her? Do you know what that's like? The constant fight-- the constant miserable struggle to move forward, inch by inch in mud and soot? All in vain. She almost appeared to be perfectly happy for a while. All pain washed away from her. We were able to have sex more often. For so long, I felt like a trespasser, in my own wife-- a trespasser. I finally began to feel as if she enjoyed the occasions. It was a dream, it really was. We defeated her trauma. I really believed it."

"I'm sorry."

"I was excited. I was truly excited, even the day it all changed. I wonder what God's purpose is behind that? Some of the greatest moments in my life were always shortly followed by the worst sufferings. I hate that. Fantastic birthdays and winters filled with luminous and simple memories, to be followed by the death of my sister. Wonderfully pleasant mornings with cool wind and spotless skies, ending with a bloodied pet under tread marks. Why does God do this?"

"I really don't know."

"Well, honestly, I wouldn't expect any profound answers from you."

I sit back on the ugly sofa and glance at him. He still keeps his head down. The weather outside continues to be miserable. It's raining heavier than ever before. I do hope the weather is a little better back home. I hope Mary can rest. I sure hope she experienced some joy today. I never got to tell her goodnight. I hope she hasn't been trying to call me. I'm an absent husband, a missing father, practically a worse thing than the evil I hunt.

"The day all of it changed." I remember where I was in my shriving, "I was excited. I was secretly hoping for a girl. I never shared that. Mary always wanted boys, and I never understood that. Girls are so sweet, for a while at least. We went to the hospital to see what we had to plan for, and the results broke Mary. Absolutely broke her. Everything we had worked towards was ruined in a single instance. She had been anxious beforehand. I assumed it was only pregnancy-related stuff. Even after I thought it was the culprit, but no. She has yet to recover, and I know those hormones can take some time to balance out, but no. She's never recovered, and frankly, I don't know if she ever will."

"Time heals many wounds."

I want to bash his face in.

"Father," I stand from the sofa and lean down in front of him. He still refuses to look me in the eyes. "Father!"

He looks up, squinting his beady eyes beneath his arrogant glasses.

"Have you ever made sexual advancements on children?"

89

"I have not." He says. He isn't lying. He hasn't.

"What about young boys?"

"No."

"Do you lust after them?"

He looks away. He's telling the truth. He has lusted.

"Have you ever looked at child pornography? How far does your attraction go?

He says nothing.

"Did it ever occur to you, maybe you're unfit for ministry?"

"You've never looked at teenage girls in any way?"

I slap him. His glasses sling from his face onto the wooden floor just beyond his rug.

"I don't entertain such things. But you, I'm sure you've heard it all as a priest, have you not?"

"I've heard everything."

"Did it desensitize you? I don't understand how you could know everyone's pain and continue with your perversions. How'd you never throw yourself off a building?"

"They're only thoughts." He defends as he sobs. The confessor is broken.

"No, you take action with your thoughts."

"I haven't!" The confession is flipped.

"You've defended predators. Father Gulli was one that I know of. I'm sure, in some way or another, your career is filled with such things. If anything, your ministry excuses them." He doesn't say anything for some time, "Father, forgive me. I have more sins to confess."

I clear my mind of his sounds of weakness and fear. I close my eyes, remembering all the dirt I've collected in my dustpan, all the other monsters. I didn't let them speak for so long. I called their numbers quickly.

"I've killed. I've murdered." The priest hears the words and shivers.

"No, no, no—" He mutters.

"There's no sense in trying to dress it differently to you. I have broken the law, whatever sort of law it may be, that pedophiles shouldn't die. I simply cannot tolerate such an absence of justice. There must be justice."

"You deprive them of the chance to repent."

"They deprive themselves of the chance, and before I ever sink my knife into them, if God is willing, they could make a perfect act of contrition."

"God have mercy on me!" He begs quietly, several times.

"Finally, father, I've sinned against you. I've harmed you."

"If you're repentant," He begins to believe he has a way out, after all, "you must let me go."

"Father, remember what we agreed on. Your only real shot at mercy is showing mercy yourself."

"Please, don't kill me. Please, please, please--"

"Father, show me the mercy you'd like to receive from God." I inch closer to him. I have the knife in my hand as I approach this tricky situation. I don't get enough practice with such priests that are possibly willing to absolve me.

"No, no, please don't! I'd surely go to Hell. Please, please don't!" His voice raises, he vainly fidgets in his bindings.

"What is my penance, father." The only part I genuinely fear. This is another point of possible failure.

"Don't kill me! I'll change! I'll teach differently!" I stuff the rag in his mouth.

"Father! This is my confession. I need you to stop making such a fuss. Please, focus, and you may have His Mercy." His muffled screaming stops. I remove the rag once again.

"The only penance I could give is to turn yourself in."

"Why? How come Father Gulli didn't have to?" He doesn't answer me. "Davis, I need to know why I can't have better mercy than a sexual predator deserved." He still does not respond.

I back away from him for a moment. Sophia smiles at me in some not so distant memory. I raise my eyebrows at her, and she tries to mimic. She tightly shuts her eyes and laughs. The little girl doesn't know how to control her eyebrows. I like to tickle under her chin, and she laughs uncontrollably. I've never felt such simple joy over anything, never in my entire life. I wish Mary wasn't so harmed—what a thing, to be broken by such a source of love. I look back to the priest. Hopefully, he's able to excuse me for the sake of my children.

"Damn it, Father! I have a family!" I'm equally hopeless. "I have children at home, and they need me. How could you damn an entire family for my actions, my sins that aren't so evil?"

There's a time of silence from his crying, snorting. There's peace from the heavy rain beating against the roof of his house. Perhaps I can live with his penance. Maybe, God will let me live long enough to at least get the kids through school. He never said that I'd have to turn myself in immediately.

"Father, I've failed to mention one more sin. I've lied to you."

"About?" He's worried that he knows. He knows correctly, and it shows.

"I'm going to kill you," He begins shouting, and I stuff the same rag into his mouth. "Father Davis, I'll make it very quick, but I need you to absolve me after it's done. You're going to be in a little bit of pain, but I need you to focus on absolving me. I'm confessing my guilt for murdering you, along with the others. Please, show me the same mercy that you've been full of all your ministry. Show me the mercy that you'd want from God." There's a strange look in a man's eyes, in his face, when he knows he's going to die. I think of animals being slaughtered, and it's not the same, yet it is. There's just something about a man dying. Maybe it's the soul, perhaps it's the sight of eternity.

He fights hard against the cables and tape tied around him. He wiggles and squirms like a worm before the hawk. I move behind him and cut his right arm, vertically, across the skin and veins. My blue glove becomes soaked in a deep dark red, almost purple in color, almost brown. He fights hard. I quickly cut the left arm, and he struggles again. I move even faster to remove his rag and hear his Absolution for all I've done.

"Why?"

"Please, Father, hurry."

To my surprise, I receive his delirious absolution as his life fades. He gives in and is emptied of his soul as his blood pours out slower and slower. I pray the Act of Contrition as I watch. His eyes look blankly into the air, just past my head. I wonder if there's any sort of activity behind them. Is he partaking in a near-death experience far in the depths of his mind? Has he already been shuffled off to Hell? It's ominous as he stares into the air as if he saw something just before going. I turn to look. I want to see his last sight, his final gaze on this earth. It's something of a ritual of mine.

I turn, following where his eyes lead, and I realize that we weren't alone.

INFERNUM

A man is sitting at the end of the couch. His head hangs, held up by hairy hands over his lap. He appears grief-stricken with his eyes closed beneath massive eyebrows, squinting in visual melancholy.

Every nerve in my body is electrifying, my blood courses, and I prepare myself to fight. Who is he? Are there others? Have I been discovered?

"Who the hell are you?" I shout at the man, with my bloodied knife held forward. It drips over the cool air, onto the rug below. I am almost ready to launch at him, but I have no desire to kill an innocent. My only war has been against the perverts.

He doesn't answer. He seems unconcerned with me. He doesn't appear to be the least bit worried that I stand with a weapon in hand.

"What are you doing here?"

He looks up and makes brief eye contact with me. His eyes, his face are familiar. I recognize him, but my mind is hazy with the shock of his presence. The man looks away from me and stares toward the empty body of the priest. He stands from the couch and begins to walk in our direction. I grip tighter around the knife. I'm only able to grip tighter. I'm powerless to move toward him; I only step back from him as he kneels down to the priest.

"Have you been following me? Who do you work for?"

"*Simon*, be silent." He bends down and closes the lifeless eyes of the priest.

"Who the hell are you? How do you know my name?"

"Of course, I know the name of the man who killed my human."

"What? *Your* human?" The words don't make any sense to me.

"I was his Guardian."

"Guardian?"

"Put the knife down, Simon."

"No! Answer me, or die with him!"

I'm immediately struck by a force, a sort of wind that blasts me against the couch and knocks the knife far from my hand, flinging it out and into the kitchen. It's as if the air in the room contained a hurricane, but only for a single instant.

"I am an Angel." His eyes contain flames. "Do not dare insult me with threats of mortal harm. If God so wills, I would vaporize you where you stand. I would reduce you to *dust*."

I watch him. That's all I'm able to do. Have I finally wandered into a psychotic-break? Has my grandmother's schizophrenia called for me? An angel? Angels look like *this*?

"No, you've not lost your mind." He speaks softly, in a tone polar opposite to the previous one.

"How—"

"None of you ever have any faith. You all compete to be the most devout, the most prayerful, most holy. When you encounter what it is you desire to see most, you're absolutely faithless. Have you been pretending? Why the shock?"

"No—no, you're the man from the plane!"

"Yes, we met on that plane." He says, teary-eyed. "But, more accurately, I was this man's guardian. I was his guardian, but no longer."

"Why? Why do you grieve for him? I don't und—"

"My only human. My sole mission. It has failed."

"Failed?"

"He's in Hell, now."

The *angel* reaches toward me with stretched fingers. I'm unable to dart away from him. His heavy hand lands gently on my forehead, and I feel sent away. My vision is static. All I see is static, like an old television receiving no transmission. The static consumes me. My thoughts, desires, and identity are lost in confusion. My every sense is filled with noise. It stops, but there is no relief to the sensation. It's as if I am within the very static, surrounded, and even made of it.

There's a heat like I've never felt, a heat, unlike a stovetop or bonfire. My very soul feels cooked; my thoughts are engulfed and consumed in it. I find myself within the dark depths of the earth. I panic and begin looking around the blackness as my very existence feels hollowed out. My every motion feels automated in a way. I try to step away and run in the opposite direction, but it's as if I'm on a sort of conveyor belt. I'm not able to move from whatever destination awaits—the temperature rises. I would say that the fiery warmth here is true heat; there's more to it than pain and degrees. The flames on earth are much more like shadows than the true nature of them in this Hell.

As I'm carried forward, I continue to vainly scramble my legs. Before me, I see *it*. My motion stops, and I find myself standing on a scorching bank. I see the vast sea of molten rock and magma. I see charred arms and blackened hands stretching out from the liquid brilliance. All sound is painful to endure, and every cry to Heaven is just as loud and deafening as the first. Their voices don't go hoarse, even after centuries of screaming.

I look out and overhead, towards what appears to be the sky. It's not a sky, but a cave ceiling covered in collected smoke and steam. It looks filled with clouds, grey and brown, and for moments it is broken and illuminated by *falling stars*. The longer I watch them, the more I'm able to perceive that *they* are not stars but phosphorous bodies combusting, clothes incinerating off of them as they fall. The *stars* shriek and curse as they make their way down and slam into the magma. Their sounds are lost in the mass of lamentations.

Something closer to me makes noise, something close to my feet. In the sizzling sands of the bank, I see a hand reaching towards my feet. The arm attached to the hand is wounded vertically; its blood boils from the opening. I step back away from it and see the owner's face. It's the priest. Around his neck is the glowing white collar that chokes him as he makes noises unlike those of humans. He attempts to communicate something to me, but I cannot understand anything aside from his anguish.

He is there.

I blink and find myself in the comforts of that living room. I feel the familiar presence of God so intensely upon my arrival that I fall from the sofa and onto my hands and knees and weep with relief. It's a sensation I'm not deserving of, to witness His presence even as it is on earth. Within the confines of torment, the feeling wasn't there; it was worse than the absence of air to breathe.

"So, yes. I am sorrowful that another is lost."

"God have mercy!"

I sit up from the floor and lean my back against the couch. I'm exhausted, my energy drained by the single instant I spent *there*.

"What have I done?"

"It's not *your* fault he is there. All souls, all people you perceived in that pit, are ones who rejected God. Father didn't *send* them there—they chose it. *You* didn't fling him there—he chose it with his years of heresy and corruptions."

"Why did you never stop me?" I become angry with the angel, "You never said anything on the plane! You slept!"

"Do not raise a temper with me. I was *unable* to do anything. My guidance, my protection, is only as good as it's allowed to be. My human did nothing of God's will. For years I tried to pull him away from dangers and damnation, but he surrendered himself to the other."

"Why are you telling me this? Why doesn't my angel?"

"Father wills what He wills. He's sanctioned me to commune with you, perhaps because He knows my anguish is so great."

"What am I to do? If I turn myself in—"

"You must do the penance given to you. You must discontinue your crusade. The law of the land does not permit it. You must be obedient to the law, as I am obedient to our Father. Do not think for a moment there weren't times I felt as you did. All of us, the entire Host of Heaven, watch humanity, even in its darkest of moments. Your place is with your children and wife. You are a sort of guardian for them—those tormenting flames of Hell attempt to seduce all souls. Without paterfamilias in the home, your family's odds of reaching paradise are critically reduced. Justice comes to all."

"*If* I turn myself in, they will be without a father."

"As such might be the cost for your sins." The angel said coldly.

My entire world is ended with his pitiless words. I think of all my love, my family. I can't for a moment, imagine not watching the little girl grow into a woman. I will miss so many things, *all* of the things. However, I think back to the image of that priest, the image seared into my mind. I know I'm not the *cause* of his being there, but the vision petrifies me. The sight is what I will be if I do nothing. The pains and torment of it all isn't even the worst part of it. That dreadful feeling or lack of feeling, that place without God, is the worst. There is no other option. For months now, I almost accepted the price of my actions. I believed I was at peace with being damned if it meant I could prevent others' suffering in this world. Mary will be broken, unquestionably, there's no recovering from this. There's no sense in any of it.

"There's no sense in any of it because you are fallen. It's all very sensible because God is sensible." He responds to my thoughts.

"Will you pray for me? Or help me? Whatever it is you all do? I don't believe I'm strong enough."

"Of course."

I do not call her. I can't bear to hear the worry in her voice if I were to wake her. I can't call them. I'm weeping in my rental car as I drive to the nearest police station. I can't believe I'm doing this.

I can't believe any of it. I'm angry at myself for having ever started down this path. I just don't understand it. I don't understand any of it. The world is unjust, yes. It was always so, at least post-Eden, it's been this way. I'm the same as an ancient man. We're made of similar things. I don't believe this world is meant to contain such people. I want to scream and kill; I don't want to sit in cubicles and apologize for my offensive words. I don't want to read articles about queer abusers and failed rehabilitation for the sickos. How could any expect a different reaction?

Where are the men at? Why have I been alone in doing this? Why are my works criminal actions and not ones demanded by society? I always thought I was doing a civic duty. I still believe it must be done, but Heaven says no. It does not compute. I know, for a fact, I know that I *can't*. I'm angry about it all, but I must deny those emotions.

My thoughts wander back to that angel I left in the priest's former home. He is a perfect being, and even he was angry with things, yet he did nothing more than God willed. That angel allowed it all to happen. He never disobeyed. That, that is the Fruit of Knowledge. That's the difference. I see it now, even with my eyes filled with tears. The angel did not know evil; he does not have the knowledge of evil as I do. He must have always seen the sin, but he never tasted its *sweetness*. He never sank his teeth into the pulp of vice, never once felt the juice spill over his lips. Never has sin dripped from his chin as it quenched his cravings. He never had an appetite for it, but I do.

The map on my phone tells me that my destination is in nine-hundred feet. My heart sinks into the pit of my chest. I'm almost nauseous as I tap the breaks to slow, to make my turn.

"God, wake me! Wake me from this nightmare, please!" I think back to when it all started. No, I couldn't ask to be woken from this. It's not all been a nightmare. I'd much rather this happen than Sophia to have never existed. It's something worth being thankful for that he doesn't fulfill our every wish.

I park in the front lot and step out into the cold drizzle. The LED lights glow from the front windows, illuminating all the microscopic droplets of water. Nothing is hidden from the lighting; all things are revealed.

I text Mary, *I love you*, there's so much to say, but those three words are all I send. I reach for the door handle and pull it open. I likely look like a wreck to the people that see me enter. They all know somethings up; there's no hiding from it now—no more hiding from any of it. I will say, whatever I feel now, this strength to do this is not my own. That angel is certainly working some graces for me.

"How can I help you?" The policeman asks from behind the desk. He looks me over, his eyes peering past his large Mediterranean nose.

"I've—" the words are heavy as stones, "I've come here to turn myself in."

"What for?" The officer asks. He stands from his chair and motions to another across the room. I've entered myself into a lion's den.

"I've killed seven priests." The words feel as if they do not belong to me. I'm dizzy; a sort of dissociative sensation comes over me. The officer appears shocked, waiting for me to share more detail.

"You *killed* the priests?" He *whispers*. There's a look on his face; I'm unsure what it means. He makes another gesture to whoever he had previously called.

I nod my head, yes.

"Wait, these the same ones from the news? The child-abusers?"

"Yes. One in San Francisco, one in Miami—"

"Shhh—" He gestures to the other cops again, and the officer steps away from the counter. I watch him as he comes around to meet me. I place my hands behind my back, together, waiting for his handcuffs. "Follow me."

I turn slowly to see him pointing *outside*. Something over his shoulder catches my gaze. On a bench sits a grungy *man*, with shaggy hair and a stubbled face. He nods his head at me and winks just as the police officer leads me outside into the drizzle. The officer looks me in the eyes as he lights a cigarette. Half of his face illuminated by the lights, the other half dim from the night sky, briefly orange from the flame on his lighter.

"Get the hell out of here," he raises his eyebrows, his tone demanding, "and never, ever come back."

"But I—"

"I see your wedding ring. You got kids?" He takes two quick puffs from the smoking cigarette.

The tip glows, reminding me of the way the priest's face appeared *there.*

"Yes, three of them."

"Go home to your family, *pissa.*" He shakes his head and taps his cigarette. The ash falls onto the damp stairs.

"I'm not playing a prank, I actua—" I try to confess again, perhaps I didn't say it right. He interrupts with another gesture.

"I'll beat you to an inch of your life if you try doing that again."

"This is my penance though, it's something I *must* do."

"Well, congratulations, dummy, you did it. Now, get the hell outta my sight."

I'm unable to move, frozen with *fear?* The adrenaline I've felt causes me to stiffen and ache.

"I don't understand."

"I'm not gonna be part of this. If you wanna quit, then quit, but I don't punish heroes."

"I'm no hero."

"And you're not much of a villain either. You did a thing people been prayin' for. We got too many deviants on these streets. Go home. I won't be the one that allows you to sit in solitary for decades." He flicks the filter out into the parking lot. "Go home."

"Thank you, thank you so much," I say. I break into tears as I think of the faces of my children, my wife, the life that I may be able to return to.

"Hey, don't *ever* mention it." He reaches out his hand for a shake. I shake hands; his grip is firm and sincere. "Now, get the hell outta here and stop tryna make a scene. Gonna get us both put in the slamma."

I look towards the police station once again. No one within seems the least bit interested. No one watches, but the grungy *man* I met on that plane trip. He stands at the window, spectating. Two massive wings beam from behind him, dazzling everything around like a flash of lightning. The officer doesn't react, and I assume I'm the only one that perceives it. There's a crack of thunder, and he vanishes.

"Thank you again," I say to the officer, but also to the angel. I turn to leave, the officer watches as I walk away, and the cold drizzle lands on my face.

I have blotted out thy iniquities as a cloud, and thy sins as a mist: return to me, for I have redeemed thee.

*
**

Tap—tap-tap-tap

Her fingers tap against my shoulders again; they now serve as reminders of my duty. *Tap—tap-tap-tap* they gently pat against my shirt. The little fingers smell of fresh fruit and flowers as the aroma escapes with every additional tap. I never forget my place, here with *her,* with *them*.

Opportunities such as these are as rare as they come, but so are the blessings God has given me, and yet, I am surrounded by them. Even in a world such as ours, with all the evil and corruption, there is still the chance of love and joy. There's the chance of redemption for those who would be damned and peace for all who suffer.